THE LEGEND OF

BASS REEVES

ALSO BY GARY PAULSEN

☀ THE LEGEND OF ☀

BASS REEVES

**BEING
THE TRUE
AND FICTIONAL
ACCOUNT OF THE
MOST VALIANT
MARSHAL IN
THE WEST**

GARY PAULSEN

WENDY
LAMB
BOOKS

Published by Wendy Lamb Books
an imprint of Random House Children's Books
a division of Random House, Inc.
New York

www.randomhouse.com/kids

Educators and librarians, for a variety of teaching tools, visit us at
www.randomhouse.com/teachers

ISBN: 978-0-375-84372-3

Book design by Trish P. Watts

Printed in the United States of America

10 9 8 7 6 5 4 3 2 1

With utmost respect

for his focus and resolve

this book is dedicated to

peace officer

David Thomas.

FOREWORD

Think of the American West as the Wild West. These phrases conjure up a vision of our past filled with mountain men and Indians, cattle drives and cowboys, desperadoes and gunfighters. But the Wild West lasted only a very short time, from perhaps 1830 to 1890. At most, sixty years.

Yet that era has had a powerful effect on our culture. Clothing, speech and the frontier mentality of that time are widespread and popular to this day. Every year, it seems, Hollywood produces a new crop of films and television programs that draw from the myths and legends of the Old West. There are even social clubs where members dress as cowboys and practice quick draw, mimicking what they believe gunfighters did.

The men of the West we now regard as legendary figures loom large in our culture, many as daring criminals, some as heroes. But actually, there weren't very many of them.

There was Kit Carson—mountain man, trapper, explorer—who was said to have been one of the first white men to reach the Rocky Mountains.

Jeremiah Johnson—another mountain man, trapper

and supposed explorer—was the inspiration for dime novels of the time and a popular film in which Robert Redford starred a hundred years later.

William F. Cody, known as Buffalo Bill—scout, Pony Express rider, hunter—was another subject of popular novels of his day. He originated the famous Wild West Show, a huge hit in America and Europe.

Wyatt Earp—a lawman who became a legend in his own day—was also a character in adventure books of his time. Ned Buntline, who wrote many of those little melodramas, commissioned the Colt firearm company to make a special long-barreled handgun that he could present to Mr. Earp.

Wild Bill Hickok—so well known back then that Buffalo Bill tried to make him a star of his show—was the focus of dime novels that featured his prowess with a gun and his courage in upholding the law. Numerous films were later made about his heroism.

William Antrim—called Billy the Kid and known for fighting in the Lincoln County War of 1878 to 1881 in New Mexico—was supposed to be a master gunfighter and tragic hero who was gunned down at the age of twenty-one. Publishers and Hollywood loved his story too.

Butch Cassidy, the Sundance Kid and the Hole in the Wall Gang were a group of train and bank robbers. Because of Hollywood, Robert Redford and Paul Newman, they've become known as raffish, almost lovable scoundrels.

The American West stretched from St. Louis, Missouri, to California and the Pacific Ocean, from Canada down to Mexico. Physically, the West was huge. But it was very small in terms of population. When it was time to look for heroes, people had to take what they could get. This might be one reason that most of these figures lose credibility when examined more closely.

Much of Kit Carson's fame came from mercilessly attacking Native American people during battles in which he led groups of poorly trained and poorly disciplined men notable for committing atrocities. He had such a big ego that he insisted on being called Colonel Carson, though he'd never been in the army.

In reality, Jeremiah Johnson was completely insane. He was known as Liver-Eating Johnson because he hunted Crow Indians and, after killing them, ate their livers raw.

Buffalo Bill Cody came closer to living up to his legend. He was a scout, an explorer and a hunter and had ridden for the Pony Express as a boy and scouted for the army in the Indian Wars, during which he truly did face a Native American warrior in man-to-man combat. But his fame was largely built on his tracking down often helpless Native Americans with the army and killing them. As a hunter, he slaughtered hundreds, if not thousands, of defenseless buffalo that stood in herds on the wide-open plains. He spent his later life starring in his own show, posing for portraits, life masks and hand molds, and promoting his legend.

Wyatt Earp could be the classic case of the legend having little to do with the truth. He had been a sort of lawman in Dodge City, Kansas, and in Tombstone, Arizona, but he was no hero. He went to Dodge City because he was a fugitive horse thief from back East. At the time, this was a hanging offense. In Dodge, he gambled and managed a string of prostitutes for the cowboys who came up there on trail drives. He stole from almost every drunk he ever arrested (and there were many) and was finally "asked" to leave town because he was known to mistreat and offend even the rough trailhands who came up with the cattle drives.

Seeking his fortune in Tombstone, Arizona, Earp engineered a showdown with a group of men who were in financial control of the little boomtown and shot them down in the famous gun battle at the OK Corral. He had arrived thinking they were unarmed and helpless, but it turned out they had weapons. Once again he gambled and managed prostitutes. He spent the last years of his life in Hollywood, manipulating his legend into a more favorable light by courting movie stars like William S. Hart and Tom Mix and publishing his own versions of the truth.

Wild Bill Hickok was a chronic alcoholic and gambler who was only in one true gunfight in his life, during which he killed a man because the fellow had won Hickok's watch in a poker game. Hickok was so incompetent that one dark night, in an alcoholic stupor, he shot and killed his own deputy, thinking the man was sneaking up on him. Hickok died drunk, shot in the back of the head while gambling in a saloon in Deadwood, South Dakota.

Billy the Kid was a shiftless coward who shot men in the back, murdered his own friends and killed a deputy who was guarding him as the man pled for his life. Billy was so afraid of being captured and punished that he wrote a letter to the governor of New Mexico saying that if the governor would pardon him, he would turn against all his friends, his so-called gang, and testify against them. He was a horse and cattle thief, a drunkard and a merciless killer who was reputed to have shot an unarmed clerk simply because Billy wanted his horse. When he was finally gunned down in Fort Sumter, New Mexico, by Pat Garrett, many thought it was a rightful end to a brutish, short and squalid little life. Today he'd probably be called a sociopath and a serial killer.

Butch Cassidy and the Hole in the Wall Gang were criminals, plain and simple, not the easygoing clan of Robin Hood–like characters we know from films and folk legend. The real men robbed banks and trains and stole cattle and horses. They were thugs who attacked unarmed men and innocent women and children. They blew up a railway express car with so much dynamite that they maimed and crippled everyone inside. Hunted and driven out of the United States, they were shot down during a grubby attempt to rob a bank in South America.

All in all, poor stock to consider when looking for role models from our frontier.

And yet . . .

And yet . . .

There was a man who truly qualified as legendary and heroic.

He was born in 1824, lived until 1910, and was the most successful federal marshal in the history of the United States. Working in the Indian Territory, he brought out thousands of fugitives. He was involved in fourteen gunfights that resulted in the deaths of his opponents. True to the mythical code of the West, he never drew first and most often let the other man shoot before he returned fire. He would ride alone into hideouts containing whole gangs of fugitives to get his man. In these attempts he was the target of hundreds of rounds of gunfire. His hat and clothes were riddled with bullets, his horses were killed, his gun belt shot off his body, boot heels shot clean away, rifles shot to pieces.

Miraculously, he was never wounded.

This man was honest and honorable. He rejected countless bribes, and when his own son killed his wife, he tracked his son down, brought him to justice and sent him to prison for life.

His name was Bass Reeves.

He was an African American.

And this is his story.

AUTHOR'S NOTE

Ever since I first heard of Bass Reeves, I have wanted to write about him, and make Bass come alive to readers.

This book moves back and forth among three sections that discuss the facts of Bass's life and times, and three imagined sections that follow him from his boyhood until he was an old man. I shaped the book this way because there was so little written about Bass Reeves in his day. Most information about him in books is based on word of mouth. There aren't many accounts to refer to beyond a few newspaper articles and records of the arrests he made. The fictional sections are based on events in Bass's life, as well as my own experiences riding, hunting and living rough in the West. The part about his boyhood is the longest because to me it was the most important part of his life, the fire that forged him.

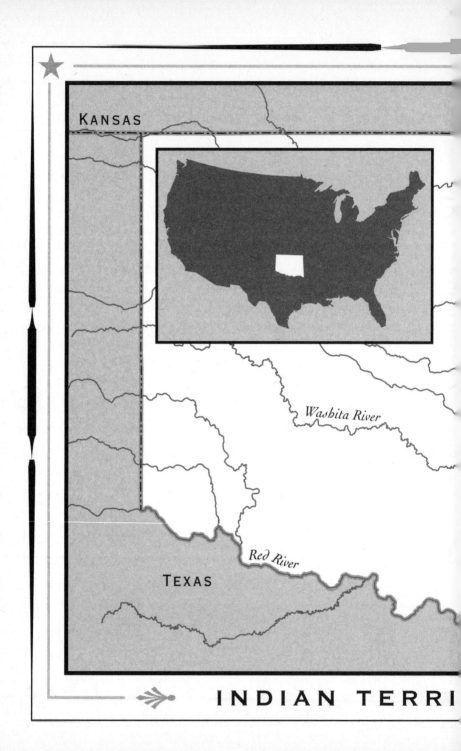

KANSAS

Washita River

Red River

TEXAS

INDIAN TERRI

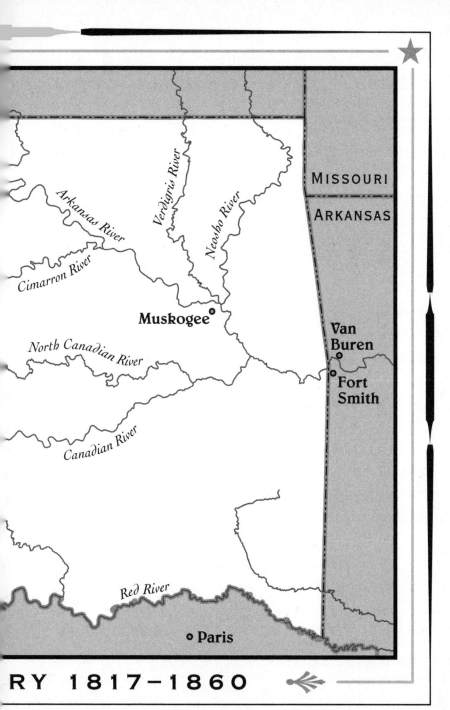

MISSOURI

ARKANSAS

Arkansas River

Verdigris River

Neosho River

Cimarron River

Muskogee

North Canadian River

Van Buren

Fort Smith

Canadian River

Red River

Paris

RY 1817–1860

❖THE LEGEND OF❖
BASS REEVES

THE BOY

1

SPRING 1834

The Witch Dog

The boy lay under a mesquite bush to get shade from the Texas sun and watched the cow intently.

She was a longhorn with horns a full five feet across. He'd seen horns that size cut men and kill horses, so he waited. She was about to go into labor, what he called getting calf sick, and when she was actually having the calf she couldn't attack him. Then he would run up, drop a noose around her head and dance back before one of those horns could catch him. The rope was twenty feet long and tied to a four-foot piece of log about five inches in diameter. When the cow tried to run, the log would tangle in the mesquite and rocks and stop her so she could be captured, branded and added to the mister's herd to sell and make him rich.

The cow moved and he studied her with a knowing eye. She was huge for a cow, with flat sides and many scars from running through brush and fighting other cows.

It would be another half hour, at least, before labor. She wasn't even hunched yet.

"You take the rope and the log," the mister had told him. The boy never thought of him as the master, though legally he was, like all white men who owned slaves. The boy's mammy had told him: "Your name is Bass, and ain't no man your master. Not now. Not ever. We got to do what we got to do 'cause of the white man's law. But that don't make no man your master in God's eyes."

Bass studied the horns. They came around so fast, and sharp, sometimes you almost couldn't see them move. Once he moved in too close on an old brindle cow and just the tip of a horn caught his trousers. Cut them open like a knife.

"*Zzzzzttt!*" The cloth almost sang. They were no-'count pants anyway, handed down from the mister, all patches and held up with a piece of tow over his shoulder. He knew his mammy would sew them up, but he didn't like the feel of the horn swinging by that close.

Another inch and I'd have been looking at my guts, he thought, squinting in the sun. Pulled out on a horn like wet rope. He'd seen cow and pig guts when they slaughtered, horse guts once when a bull hooked a mare that wasn't paying attention. He did not want to see his own.

Now he heard movement in the mesquite off to the right and waited. Might be the mister sneaking to see if he was working. Make sure he was doing.

No need at all, he thought. I work all the time. Not for the mister. I work because it makes the time pass.

It was two coyotes, low on their bellies. They knew there would soon be afterbirth for them to eat.

Bass watched them. They did not know he was there, back in the shady hole where he'd had to scare out a rattlesnake. The snake had buzzed some and then left when he pushed it with a stick. He didn't like snakes. He wasn't afraid of them—how could you be scared of something that couldn't crawl faster than a slow walk?—but they were always mad. Seems like they bit just to be mean. His mammy told him of one that crawled in a cradle and bit a baby and killed it. Why? Baby wasn't doing a thing. Sometimes Bass killed snakes, especially around the house where they could get a dog or cat or baby pig or a chicken. But when he was out in the mesquite or down at the creek bottom, he let them be. If, he thought, they let me be. He didn't like killing things without a good reason.

The mister, now, would take his percussion pistol and shoot anything. Lizards off a rock, songbirds off a rail. Or try to. Whenever he got hold of a whiskey jug, he couldn't hit the ground, let alone a bird on a fence.

Now, it was something, how the coyotes knew when a cow was ready. Maybe the smell, Bass thought, or they might be witch dogs. His mammy told him that, back in New Orleans where she was from, there were witch dogs that could tell you things if you knew how to understand them. She didn't know how to talk to the dogs but her mammy could do it, could give a witch dog molasses, and when it wrinkled its lips to lick the molasses off its tongue, she could tell if someone was going to die or when they would have a baby, and was it a boy or a girl.

"Mammy said the power skips," Bass's mammy told him. "Didn't come to me, but maybe to you, to read the

5

witch dogs. Mostly women have it, but I didn't have a girl and won't be no more chirrun. So if it happens, it will have to be you."

Bass was seven when his mammy told him that, better than three years ago come fall. He had lifted a jug of black-strap molasses from the pump house and tried it on one of the mister's old tick hounds. He tried it so often the dog took a liking to it and followed him around all day, waiting to have his tongue wiped with molasses.

Problem was, Bass remembered now as he watched the coyotes move toward the cow, problem was it gave the hound the black skoots. Dog messed the yard and the pump house and all over the porch, and Bass had to quit because the mister said he was going to shoot the hound if he didn't stop messing.

Bass never learned anything from the hound but that it liked molasses and had a straight pipe for a gut. It was a good dog and Bass felt bad when one day a snake cooling itself by the pump house bit it between the eyes. Killed that hound. After that, whenever Bass saw a snake in the yard, he would get a hoe and chop it and feed it to the pigs.

There. The cow hunched. Her labor was starting. Bass gathered the rope and the log. The coyotes saw him and one looked straight into Bass's eyes and moved its lips.

At first he couldn't believe what he saw. The coyotes were thirty-five yards away, just past the head of the cow, but when Bass shook his head, the coyote was still looking at him, straight up into his eyes. And the animal's lips moved.

Things will change.

Bass wasn't sure if he heard it or felt it like a touch on

his skin, but the phrase was there. In his head. As clear as if somebody had said it aloud. And it came from the coyote.

Things will change.

"What will change?"

He said it so loud that the coyotes both jumped and the cow started and turned to see him for the first time, though she didn't move, couldn't move now that her labor had begun.

The coyotes didn't answer him, either aloud or in his head, but they didn't run. Instead they stood, one looking at the cow, the other staring directly at Bass.

"Are you a witch dog?" Bass said.

The question hung there until the coyote turned slowly and deliberately to look at the cow.

The cow.

It was time. The mister said Bass had to get one cow a day on a tangle rope, and the sun was going down fast in the west. He held the log under his arm, readied the rope, and just as the cow started to push the calf out, he rose and ran past her head, dropping the noose neatly over her horns as she swung to hook him, but missed him because she couldn't move her body fast enough to match the swing.

The loop tightened and the hemp bunched at the bottom of her horn, against her head. It would stay and tighten when she tried to move through the mesquite later.

Still the coyotes did not run. They waited for the afterbirth, or the calf if it was born dead. Bass walked up the small rise, heading toward home.

Evening sun was coming, and though it was still hot, he could feel a coolness through the heat. Off a mile was the mister's homestead—five adobe mud huts with sod and grass roofs laid out in a rough circle. There was a mesquite fence around the outside to hold stock in, or Comanches out if they came to raid. Bass had never seen them, but had heard talk. Everybody feared them, even the mister with his rifle and pistol.

It wasn't much of a ranch. His mother had told him of plantations around New Orleans where even the slave quarters were better than the mister's adobe shack. But this was all Bass knew. The mister had won Bass's mother in a poker game in Austin when she was pregnant with Bass, and she had come here with the mister a month before her due time. Something had gone wrong and she had nearly died when Bass was born. Now she could have no more children. Luckily Bass had been born healthy and big.

The mister only had one other slave, Flowers, an old man who was nearly blind. There was something wrong in his head because he couldn't talk. He spent most of his time splitting wood and fixing harnesses. Sometimes, when a harness didn't need fixing, he would tear it apart and put it together again. He was nice enough to Bass, but mostly ignored him like he ignored everything.

As he walked into the small yard, Bass saw Flowers splitting wood. Then he trotted to the pump house near the mud hut where he and Mammy and Flowers lived and slept.

Bass drank with the slave dipper. The water was cool from the well, almost sweet, and he drank until his stomach was tight and full. Then he went to the mister's hut and called into the door.

"Mister, Mister, it's Bass."

His mammy came to the opening. She had corn flour on her hands and she wiped them on her sack apron and smiled down at him. "The boss is gone, little boy. What do you want with him?"

"Where did he go?"

"He doesn't tell me where he goes. He just saddled a horse and left. Could be he won't be back today. Could be the Comanches'll get him and we'll never see him again."

"Did he take the bay mare or the Roman nose?"

"What difference does it make?"

"If he took the bay, he'll be gone a long time. She's got good wind and a long trot. The Roman nose is strong but jerk-gaited and will wear you out on a long run."

"You talk like you ride yourself, little boy."

"I do. When nobody is looking."

"You stay off the mister's horses. He'll nail you to the door and whip you pink. You know the colored ain't to ride nothing except plugs and old mules—nothing higher than the mister."

Bass knew the rules. Well, not all of them. The whole list of rules governing slaves and masters filled books that he couldn't read. No slave was allowed to read, so how could they know all the rules? But Bass knew plenty. No slave could be in a position where the master had to look up at him. No slave could run in front of a master unless ordered to do so. No slave could eat before a master did. No slave could speak unless spoken to. No slave could walk on a sidewalk with a master. No slave could eat with the same utensils as the master. No slave could drink from the same dipper, sit on the same furniture, sleep in the same bed, wear better clothes, be close enough to exhale air into the master's lungs . . . on and on and on.

White men called it law. But even at ten years old Bass knew better. Mammy said the true law come down from God, from a man named Moses on the Mountain, and the law was for everybody, even slaves.

What white men had were just rules.

Rules to keep the colored down. And you didn't have to obey them unless you were being watched. Bass rode horses when nobody was looking. Sometimes at night when the mister was drunk asleep, he would take the bay or the Roman nose for a ride in the moonlight. Out and out, away from the homestead, riding bareback so there wouldn't be saddle marks in the morning for the mister to find, out across the sandy prairie in the silver light, the wind on his face and the powerful muscles of the horse driving him forward, driving him away, free and free and free . . .

"The bay or the Roman nose?"

"He took the bay."

"Then he's gone long. Maybe overnight. Probably went to Paris to court that widow woman."

"How do you know so much?" His mother shook her head, but the smile widened and she could not hide her pride. "You talk like you know everything there is to know in the whole world."

"I just look and see. I know he's courting because he puts that stink water on him of a morning. Won't do him no good, but he keeps trying."

"Why won't it do him any good? He's got some money,

and lord only knows how many cattle you've tangled for him. Seems like he'd be a good one to marry."

"I heard that visiting ranger say, 'He's too close to the jug,' when he came by, and that the widow Plunkett would never marry a drinker, 'cause that's what killed her first husband. And mister, he does take the jug."

"Every night," Mammy said. "I didn't think there was that much whiskey in the world. Now, you run along. I'm making corn bread with bacon grease and I'll call you when it's done. You get me some good dry wood for the stove and I'll give you a drop of honey on a slab of bread."

Bass ran off for the woodpile by the pump house, shaking a stick to scare out any snakes. Then he ate the corn bread, so hot that the honey melted like butter and soaked into it. They didn't have a cow to get milk for butter, but Mammy saved all the bacon and pork drippings in a jar, and she had smeared the drippings on the hot corn bread to mix with the honey.

"Your cooking"—Bass stood in the kitchen door, grease on his hands and face, honey in his mouth—"it must come from heaven."

"I bet you want another piece." Mammy smiled. "And maybe a slice of pork belly."

She handed him another chunk of bread and a slab of pork, mostly rubbery hot fat, the way he liked it. He went to the shade side of the hut to squat and eat.

When he was done he wiped his mouth with the back of his hand, wiped his hands on his pants and went to the pump house for a drink of cool water.

It was evening and he had sundown chores. There were hogs to feed, wood to gather for coffee and breakfast in the morning, water to carry for the Roman nose and the mules. He worked steadily, using the large wooden bucket to carry water to the troughs. He did this every night and every morning, and he didn't need to think about it while he worked, so his mind wandered back to the day with the cow and the coyotes.

Things will change.

It was there the minute he stopped thinking about anything else. He muttered to himself, "Of course things will change." Nothing stood still. But he knew the coyote's words meant more than that and when he was done with chores and had eaten again, he told his mother, "Coyote talked to me today."

They were sitting at the front of the slave quarters and she was sipping a cup of water with just a touch of the master's whiskey in it ("For my bones," she said) while they watched the sun go down. If the mister was there, they had to keep working until full dark when he went in to sleep. He didn't like to see them resting. But when he was gone, they'd sit like this and talk until it was time for bed.

"Coyotes talk all the time," Mammy said. "We hear them every night yakking and cakking down by the bottoms. They don't mean nothing by it."

"No. It's not like that. I was waiting on the cow and there was two of them and one of them kept looking into my eyes. I don't know how but his lips moved and I heard what he said inside, in my head."

Mammy believed in God and Moses on the Mountain and God's Dearly Loved Son, Jesus, with all her heart and soul but, at the same time, she knew the value and truth of signs and omens.

"What did he say to you?" She put her cup down and

held his face in her hands. "What were his words, his 'zact words?"

" 'Things will change.' "

"For the better? For the worse? Did he say?"

Bass shook his head. "No more. The words came into my head just like that, not up or down, good or bad. 'Things will change.' Then he went back to watching the cow. He didn't say more."

Mammy thought for a time. "He's talking about a good change. You're young, very young, to be talking to witch dogs, and they don't never say bad things, bad omens, to the young. It's always about something good when they talk to babies."

"I ain't no baby."

"You'll always be my baby." The sun dropped the last bit below the horizon and they were in warm, soft spring darkness. She hugged him tightly. "You live to be ninety, you'll still be my baby."

"No baby can tangle them cows, ride that Roman nose."

"Hush, boy. Don't sass your mammy."

"I'm not sassing. I'm just saying, no baby can tangle cows, ride that old jerk-gaited Roman nose the way I can."

"I know. I know. Tomorrow morning I'll make a pot of some of that Chinee tea the mister got in a silver tin box and look at the leaves. They might tell me what the omen means."

"It means a thing is going to change."

"Omens are funny and sometimes talk sideways and don't always mean what they say." Mammy stood, slowly easing her back straight, stretching the pain out. Flowers came out of the darkness and walked past them into the

13

quarters without speaking, holding a piece of harness he had been working on. He slept back in the rear corner in a small room made by stretching two pieces of canvas out from the walls. Bass and Mammy's rope cots were at the other end of the building. Flowers went to bed with the sun, got up with the sun. Bass had never heard him utter a sound except to grunt once when a mule stepped on his bare foot. He didn't even dream, it seemed, or make sounds in his sleep. Not even snoring.

"How come Flowers don't talk, Mammy?"

"Nobody knows," she said. "All I know about him is that he came from a very hard place back in Georgia where he was whipped and beaten, and it made the thinking part of his brain shut down. The mister traded six goats for him just to have him split wood and work leather."

"Were you ever whipped?"

"Not whipped. Tapped a couple of times when I was a young one like you for not knowing my manners. But not whipped, thank God."

"I ain't going to be whipped either." No one, he thought, no man will ever lay a whip to me, no man will ever turn me into something like Flowers.

"Lord, I hope not. Whipping and branding are like bad dogs coming after you." She pulled him to his feet. "Come in to bed now. It ain't good to go to sleep with bad thoughts in your head. Think on pretty things like the sunset, like corn bread and honey and cool springwater on a hot day. The days are getting longer and the sleeping time is shorter, and you need rest to grow." She said the last sentence the way she used to sing to him when he was a baby going to sleep.

The days are getting longer
And the nights are getting shorter.
Hush, little baby, don't you cry,
Mammy's going to love you by and by....
All my trials, Lord, soon be over ...

She made up songs, letting her voice, deep and soft, move around the words. He stood and followed her inside. He crawled into his bed, but sleep didn't come for a long time.

Somewhere outside, far off, a coyote sang. Another answered closer, and then eight or ten of them started yipping. He tried to listen to see if his witch dog was there with a message. But all he heard was a bunch of coyotes.

Silly old witch dog saying dumb words.

Things will change.

And his own sleep song came into his thoughts, round words rolling through his mind:

The sun came up,
   the sun went down,
And all the clouds
   went round and round....

How could things not change?

Then sleep.

2

SPRING 1836

Eagle Flying Free

He was twelve years old. Coming on to be a man. Time to think and do in man's ways. That was why he went farther than usual from the homestead looking for rabbits.

There was a creek that went past the edge of the buildings and meandered south. It was never more than a couple of feet across, more a trickle than a creek, but the damp soil along the edges made for thick willow and mesquite growth.

The brush was much wider than the creek itself, fifty to sixty yards on each side of the wet mud, and so thick it was almost impossible to move a horse through it. A boy on foot was another matter, and Bass viewed the thick green world as his own. The mister never came into the mesquite and willow because, being the only good cover in the vast expanse of the prairie, it not only attracted hordes of game—rabbits, sage hens, wild little javelina pigs—but snakes as well. Water moccasins and rattlers. The mister was mortally terrified of them.

"That creek bottom is full of devil serpents!" he'd say when he was drunk. Now that the widow Plunkett had taken up and married another man who did not drink, the mister only went to Paris to replenish his whiskey supply. He bought barrels and poured it from the barrels into a clay jug that he sipped from. As he drank more, he did less, until Mammy just about ran the homestead. She depended on Bass more each day. The mister did not allow the slaves to eat beef, and only gave them the belly fat and none of the good cuts when he slaughtered pigs, so Mammy had Bass hunt for game along the bottom. She put in a green garden down where the creek passed the horse pens and they got vegetables there, but the meat came from Bass.

Bass wasn't allowed to have a gun. The mister was as afraid as anybody of having armed slaves, so Bass had to snare rabbits and sage hens, or kill them with a Jesus stick, which was two sharpened hard willow throwing sticks tied together in the middle with rawhide to make a cross.

Bass learned to use a sidearm motion to spin-flick the Jesus stick out so hard that sometimes when he hit a rabbit, he drove it sideways and pinned it to the ground. He became good enough to hit the sage hens on the fly. Usually they were stupid and sat there and waited for him to hit them, but if they flew and he got one, it would be dead when it fell to the ground.

The rabbits nearly always screamed when they were

hit or snared, almost like a baby crying, his mammy said. The screams brought in other predators—coyotes, snakes or bobcats, and, strangely, the javelina pigs. The pigs were short-coupled, gray, covered with bristly hair, and could run very fast. They didn't seem afraid or concerned when they came upon Bass. They were also very good to eat.

The pigs were too big to be killed with the throwing stick, so Bass made a spear, or killing lance. He fire-hardened the point, and after several attempts finally managed to pin a pig to the ground, not by throwing the lance but by lunging at the pig as it ran by. Mammy cut little chops and roasts and then cooked the bits and bones with beans, and they could eat that pig with corn bread for a week and a half. Even Flowers grunted with pleasure.

But a rabbit only lasted one meal, and three prairie chickens were also a meal, and it was hard to get a javelina without a gun. Soon Bass had hunted the nearby bottoms until all the game he could get was gone. He took snakes, finally, hunting them with a stick and a hoe to cut their heads off. He stripped the skin like he was peeling fruit, cut the guts out, and Mammy cooked the meat in bean stew with peppers from the garden.

It was good meat, but the mister didn't eat it. Any good beef, any good pork, he kept for himself, and he gave the necks and feet and backs of chickens to the slaves and ate the rest. He ate white bread made with flour he bought in town. He got fat, so fat he had to use the wagon and hardly ever rode the bay or the Roman nose.

As Bass searched for game he had to move further away, until on some hunts he was five or six miles down- or upstream from the homestead.

The mister wouldn't let him take anything to ride, not even one of the stove-up mules. Thick as the mesquite was, Bass wouldn't have been able to ride the mule in the brush anyway. But he could have used it to get down to where he was going to hunt, and when he got something, he could have had the mule to carry it home for him. The day he got a javelina, he had to carry it draped across his back nearly six miles and didn't get home until midnight.

Mammy was terrified. "I thought you ran."

"What do you mean, 'ran'?"

"Ran to freedom."

He thought about that. "Where is that, freedom?"

"There are places where they don't have slaves."

"Where?"

"I'm not sure. They say follow the Drinking Gourd, which the mister calls the Big Dipper, and that's north, so it must be up north. I guess you go north till they don't have people owning other people."

"I wouldn't leave you, Mammy." He couldn't imagine living without her. "You know I couldn't do that."

"I know, little boy. I know. But sometimes things happen, and like that witch dog told you, things change. You remember I looked in the Chinee tea leaves and they said that same thing too."

"Well, I wish the change could be Mister giving me a gun and a mule to ride. Even a little shooter. I could get one of those spring deer if I had me a gun."

But in a way it was just as well he didn't have a mule.

If he'd been riding, the Comanche would have seen him and he'd be dead.

They nearly got him anyway.

It was a hot day and he'd gone nearly seven miles

downstream hunting. The mister no longer had Bass tangling the wild cows because he was too fat to ride out and drag them in, so there were plenty of cows along the banks in the mud and mesquite.

Bass had thought of spearing a good-sized calf, but the danger of actually trying to do battle with a longhorn's calf, when the mother could pick up a horse on her horns and gut it, made him reconsider. Besides, he wouldn't be able to get the meat home.

So he had kept moving along the creek, threading his way through the mesquite until he was in new territory and he started to see more game. He'd missed two throws with the Jesus stick when he suddenly came into an opening, a trail that crossed the creek.

It wasn't over ten feet at the widest. It came from the north and crossed to the south and seemed like a well-used trail. Bass had heard tales of buffalo migrating, so at first he thought it might have been a place where they came through. How hard would it be to kill one of them without a gun? Probably at least as hard as killing a longhorn. He had thought of somehow making a bow and arrows. But he never could find the right wood for a bow and they always broke. He was thinking about this when he noticed two things.

One, all the tracks on the trail that came through the mud from the north to the south were horse tracks.

Two, none of the tracks showed horseshoes. All the hoofprints were bare hooves.

For almost a minute he was excited. There were wild horse herds just as there were wild cattle. He hadn't seen them but he knew they existed. If this was a place where wild horses crossed, he might be able to use a rope to make a trap, catch a young horse and break it to ride. Would the slave laws apply if a slave actually captured a wild horse and tamed it for himself? Then he remembered that Mammy had told him that no slave could own any property. It always belonged to the mister, so even if he captured a horse and broke it, in the end the horse would belong to the fat drunkard.

He stopped thinking when he heard a strange sound. He had been in the willows and mesquite so long now that every motion, every sound, was familiar. This was new, something hitting metal. It came from the north on the trail. He had a sudden thought that this wasn't a wild horse trail at all, but one used by ridden horses, and that some men were coming, perhaps Texas Rangers. He knew how rough these men were, especially with Mexicans or slaves, and he moved back into the mesquite. Then, in the same thought, he remembered that all white men rode horses that had been shod.

These were tracks without horseshoe prints.

Only Indians rode horses without shoes.

And the only Indians to come into this country were Comanches. He had never actually seen a Comanche, but he had heard tales of what they did and none were good.

He moved further back to crouch in the shadows. He held his breath and waited. Whoever it was, he prayed that the horses wouldn't smell him and alert the riders.

Minutes crawled by like hours. Bass realized he had been holding his breath and he let it out slowly, took another. Back in the brush he heard no further sound. He was on the edge of thinking he had been wrong when he saw it: a splash of red moving past a small opening in the leaves. Just there, and gone.

He lowered his head to the ground to a spot where the brush hadn't grown, and he saw it.

It was a white Indian pony with a bright red hand about twice life-size painted on its left front shoulder. Sitting on the horse was a Comanche warrior, painted for war with black stripes on his upper body and black and white stripes on his cheeks and around his eyes. He carried a small shield made of buffalo hide with the same red hand painted on it, and he held the shield and a killing lance in one hand and a rope rein tied to the horse's jaw in the other. Except for leather leggings and a breechclout he was naked, with his shoulders and arms greased to keep flies and mosquitoes away. Across his back was a small quiver with eight or ten arrows and a short bow.

He stopped in the middle of the little creek and let his horse drink. In spite of the heat it did not take much water. It turned its head and seemed to look directly at Bass. Then it turned away, slobbering water to cool its lips and mouth.

Bass knew he should be terrified—Comanches were said to eat the hearts of their victims, cutting them out alive—but he could not feel any fear. That would come later.

Instead there was almost overwhelming awe. He felt like he was looking at some . . . some wild being that had never been broken, never been tamed.

Never been owned.

A wild thing that was and had always been free.

Free.

The Comanche turned and looked around carefully, stopping Bass's heart as his eyes swept over the hiding place. When his head turned, Bass saw he had a long black braid down the middle of his back. One perfect eagle feather was tied into the braid.

He's an eagle, Bass thought, an eagle flying free.

Nobody could tell this man whether he could own a horse or not, where he could sleep, what he could eat. Somebody might come along and kill him, or he might kill them.

But they'd never own him.

The Comanche raised his hand, signaled forward, then pulled his horse's head up out of the water and moved out of sight. There was a moment of silence, then more horses and warriors appeared.

There were eight, all dressed for war with decorations on their horses. They looked as wild and fierce as the leader, and when they had watered their horses and moved on and left Bass sitting back in the brush, when they were gone, Bass felt the first jolt of numbing fear.

Comanches. A raiding party of Comanches dressed for war, and Bass had heard many tales of what such a war party might, would probably do. They were heading south. Mammy and the homestead were to the northeast, at least seven miles in what should be a safe direction.

But the raiding party could loop north, and there wasn't anything to stop them but Mammy, old Flowers and the mister, who couldn't hit a barn wall.

Bass set off at a run to warn them, knowing that it would take him nearly an hour to get there.

An hour of not knowing, not seeing, not hearing as he ran, barefoot, eyes down to watch for snakes and cactus. He ran at a dead lope for over a mile until his wind gave out; then, a fast trot.

He had to warn Mammy.

3

SPRING 1836

Blood Moon

Now he had a gun.

When the mister heard about the raiding party, he was so afraid that he even gave a little shooter to twelve-year-old Bass. It was a .36-caliber percussion-cap muzzle-loading rifle with a barrel almost as long as Bass was tall. The mister showed him how to pour a little measured powder from a powder horn down the barrel, then take a small piece of rag for a patch across the muzzle, then a round ball, and use the ramrod to slide it down onto the powder.

He showed Bass how to take a cap from a tiny metal box, put it on the nipple, cock the hammer back, aim at a piece of firewood on the ground about thirty feet away and pull the trigger.

There was a crack, a mild punch against Bass's bare

shoulder and a great cloud of smoke. When it cleared, the firewood had been knocked over and there was a rip down the side where the ball had torn the wood.

"You ain't never shot before?" the mister asked, casting a skeptical eye at the gouged wood. "When I wasn't around?"

"No sir, Mister. First time." But not, Bass thought, the last. I get me one of these and we'll eat like those kings in the Bible Mammy is always talking about. I'll be able to kill anything that walks, crawls or swims.

"Might be you're a natural." Mister shook his head, not believing it. He knew the slaves lied to him. All the time. He saw Mammy talking to the boy sometimes and when he came up they would quit and make up something to be busy about. "If the Comanche come, you wait until they're really close, and I mean so you can see the spit when they scream like they do when they hatchet people. Then you aim at the biggest part and pull the trigger. Then reload as fast as you can, if you can, and shoot again. Keep shooting until they kill you. You work from the quarters. I'll be in the main house."

With that he went into the main house and closed the doors.

"I ain't never seen Comanches," Mammy said, "but I knew a woman who said she saw a white family lying by the road with so many arrows in them it looked like hair."

She was at the pump filling buckets. "You take these into the quarters. Should they come, we'll need water. Flowers! Come haul buckets."

Flowers ignored her, and Bass took the water into the quarters. Whoever had built them had understood the need for safety and there was only one door, made of thick boards of cottonwood. The three small windows had heavy wooden shutters that could be closed and barred from the inside.

It was early evening when they got all the water and a full ham from the smokehouse into the quarters. Then they sat.

And waited.

And waited.

Into the dark night, sitting awake until the moon came up. Flowers went to bed. Bass wasn't sure that the man even understood what they were waiting for. In any event, he didn't seem to care and was soon sound asleep.

Bass and Mammy sat on the bench by the door in the dark, now and then sipping cool water and whispering.

"Why are the Comanches so mean?" Bass asked. "We never done anything to them."

"Not the colored. It's the whites they got a mad on for, near as I can figure. But we belong to the whites so they kill us, too, I reckon. Like they kill the whites' horses, cows, pigs. They even kill chickens. Then they burn everything." She shook in the darkness. "They say they burn folks as well, burn them alive just to hear them scream. That'd be terrible, just terrible. . . . Listen, you got to promise me one thing."

"What, Mammy?"

"If they come and it looks . . . bad, looks like we ain't going to come out the other side . . . promise me you'll run."

"Run where?"

"Away. You either go on foot and hide or you take one of the mister's horses and you ride away as fast as you can and you don't look back and you don't listen back. Just cut and run. Get away."

"I ain't leaving you!"

"You have to. Worst thing for a mother to know is that her chirrun die before she does. Don't do that to me. You get away. Run north, south, wherever you can. But you run. Promise me."

He was silent.

"Promise me now or I'll thump you."

"Mammy, if it looks like we can't fight them, I'll run."

"Promise. Cross fingers and spit on the ground promise."

And finally he did. But even with the cross fingers and spit promise he thought, I will stay. I got me a gun now.

All through the long night they waited. Finally they dozed, until daylight, when the mister came out and ran to the side of his house and puked whiskey, and Flowers came out and sat down and started working on leather.

The Comanches didn't come. Not then, and not the next night or the next, and finally on the third day, they let down their guard.

That night the riders came.

Not Comanches, but white men. There were twelve of them, about half of them Rangers, hard men riding lathered horses. Bass saw two black men riding with them. Both the black men were carrying rifles but riding plow mules. The mules were so foamed up they looked like they were covered in soap, and when they drank they almost staggered to the trough.

A tall, thin man with a thick mustache pulled his horse in front of the main house. "Come out, Murphy!"

The mister came to the door, clearly drunk. "What do you want?"

"The Alamo has been destroyed, every man killed! We're going against Mexico! Bring your stock and your coloreds."

The mister stood staring at him. "What's the Alamo?"

"God, man! Where have you been? This is war! We're fighting for the Republic! Santa Anna is on the march and we have to fight him. . . ."

He trailed off because the mister turned away and went back inside the house. The man whirled, looked at Bass and Mammy and Flowers, started to say something, then shook his head, swore and rode off. The rest of the men followed and the blacks on the mules weaved and staggered as their exhausted mounts responded to kicks and whips.

Bass felt a strange excitement that he didn't understand. "What's the Alamo, Mammy?"

"I don't know."

"What's Mexico?"

"It's a place south. They eat beans and some kind of flat bread made with corn flour ground fine. I don't think those people get this far north very often."

"Are we going to have a war?"

"I don't think so. Wars are mostly what white folks do when they want something. Or that's the way it looks to me. All I know is that the Comanches didn't come, and the mister is too drunk to cause trouble or take you off to fight, and for that I thank Moses on the Mountain and God's little boy Jesus. . . . Now, fetch wood and we'll cook up some food and then get some sleep. We been three days without sleeping in our beds."

That night Bass dreamt in swirls of action and color. There were Comanches with eagle feathers, and the men on sweaty horses and the black men with rifles all shooting at each other, falling as bullets hit them, only to stand up again.

He awakened before daylight and went outside, listening. There was nothing but the normal early-morning birdsongs. He took a piece of corn bread with bacon grease from the quarters stove, and the rifle and a small sack with the powder horn and some extra balls and caps, and tiptoed out into the dawn. It was good that the Comanches seemed to have gone on in some other direction, but they still bothered him. He decided to head back down to the creek where the crossing was to see what he could find.

Could he take a horse or a mule? The mister was so drunk he wouldn't know. But Bass was going to take the rifle, and keep it until told to give it back, and if the mister did wake up or come outside and saw both a horse and the rifle gone, he might act up.

So Bass went on foot. It was a cool morning and the rising sun felt warm on his back as he jogged along. He was there in just over an hour. He had run up alongside the willows and mesquite to stay out of the thickest part, and when he approached the crossing, he moved back into them, slowed, and came up on the crossing easily, trying to be quiet.

There were horse tracks in the mud, going the other way, the same unshod hooves. The Comanches had come back in the last three days. He stood, looking at the track, wondering what they had done, what they had seen, which ranches, if any, they had attacked and burned.

A slight noise alerted him and he turned to see three javelina come to the creek not twenty feet away. Two of the little pigs went down to drink and a bigger one stayed up on the rise, looking at him. Bass had gone a long time without wild pig, and without thinking he raised the rifle, aimed and fired.

The morning stillness was absolutely shattered by the crack of the shot. He couldn't believe how loud it sounded. Birds flew up, a deer that had been in the willows crashed away, and smoke seemed to billow out in a great cloud.

The pig was dead. Bass had hit it in the head, though slightly off center. He had an old short piece of butcher knife the mister had thrown away. It was so honed down it was only four inches long, but very sharp. He cut the pig open and scooped the guts out.

He hurried, pushed by the loudness of the shot and hunger to get fresh meat back to Mammy. In just moments he had wiped the carcass out with fresh grass, thrown it over his shoulder and stood to climb away from the creek, when he saw two things.

First, right in front of him in the soft grass next to the little creek there was a hoofprint heading north, up away from the creek. It was an unshod print, like all the rest, and would not have been notable except for one vital point: it was slowly filling with water. The hoof that had made the print had passed this way not five minutes earlier. And Bass had just fired the rifle. The hair went up on the back of his neck and he turned to move back into the brush as deeply as possible. Then he saw the second terrifying vision.

The same Comanche warrior he had first seen, drawn by the sound of the shot, had just come over the rise not forty yards away, his horse cantering easily.

Bass froze; he felt his bowels loosen and an almost uncontrollable urge to run.

But his legs didn't move.

He stood staring as the warrior raced up to him and stopped his horse so fast, it slammed back on its haunches and then stood, trembling, nostrils flared.

The horse stared at Bass with the same fierce look as the Comanche.

The Indian sat studying Bass.

And Bass thought, I didn't reload my rifle.

The Comanche raised his lance and shook it in the air.

Bass saw the two fresh scalps hanging from the steel point, bloody little circles of skin with the hair hanging down. Long hair, from women or girls. One was yellow and the other a reddish color.

When the Indian saw that Bass had seen the scalps, he heeled his horse so hard it grunted and lunged forward. He touched Bass with the end of the lance, slapped Bass's neck with the flat side of the point. He screamed and whirled his horse and streaked off over the hill, making a kind of high-pitched yipping.

Bass almost fainted. He had been so sure the lance was going to go through him. He sank to the ground and stared after the vanishing Indian.

He had no thoughts at all, not even relief that he was still alive.

Then it all rushed in on him and he started shaking and didn't stop until he had carried the pig carcass nearly half a mile. He walked in wonder, trying to figure why the Comanche hadn't killed him. The Indian hadn't had a rifle and people had said that Indians all carried rifles.

But to touch him that way, with the point of his lance, and then ride off screaming? It didn't make any sense. When he got back to the ranch and told Mammy about it, she was furious.

"I told you not to go down there!"

"No you didn't, Mammy. Besides, I had me a gun and he didn't hurt me anyway. Like I said, he just—"

"I shouldn't have to tell you. You know I don't want you to go chasing after no Comanche. You know what I want and don't want and you did it anyway. You'll be lucky if I don't take a skillet and slam the brains outta your head. Hummph! No problem there, ain't got no brains."

She went on like that while she skinned the wild pig but finally she hugged him and started cooking. He ate greasy meat until he was full and it was evening.

The mister called Mammy up to the main house to cook his supper. After he had eaten and Mammy had returned to the quarters, Mister came out and called for Bass. He took the gun away.

"Your mammy said you ran into a Comanche again."

"Yes sir. I was down to the crossing and used the gun to take me a wild pig, and the Indian heard it go off and came running at me on a horse. Then he stopped, and didn't stick me with that big sticker they carry, he only touched me with it, with the point end. There was two skins on the end."

"Skins—you mean scalps?" Mister stood up straighter.

"Yes sir. There was a yellow one and a reddish one. Looked like they come from women."

"Yellow and red . . ." Mister thought, rubbing his face. He wasn't so drunk after a big meal. "That might be the Garnetts. Betty Garnett had long blond hair and her daughter had reddish hair. Garnett was riding with those men that want to go to war with Mexico. Lord, Lord!"

Bass looked suddenly at him. He thought Mister had been too drunk to know what the men had said before.

"I bet he wishes he had stayed home now. Get up early tomorrow and saddle the bay. We'll ride over there and see if anything needs tending."

"You want me to ride too?"

"Take a mule with a packsaddle. You can ride in back of the saddle. Oh, and pack a shovel and pick and tell Mammy we'll want some vittles to take with us. . . ." He turned and went back into the house. Bass went back to the quarters and told Mammy what to do.

"I should go too," she said. "Might need a woman's touch when it comes to tending . . . he won't let me go, though. Listen, should there be a need for burying, you see that they look nice and you say a prayer over them. I don't think the mister will do it so you'll have to. Can you do that?"

"I don't really know a burying prayer."

"Just say our day prayer. The one I made you learn by memory? Make sure you do it and make the sign of the cross, or those poor souls will have to wander forever."

"Wander where?"

"Between heaven and . . . never mind. Just do as you're told so they'll have peace in their souls." She sighed. "It probably don't matter. The mister, he'll drink and forget you're going."

They went to bed with dark and Bass slept hard but dreamt again of the Comanche riding with eagle feathers flying, except this time the horse was streaking red flames down his sides and two little girls were running in front of the warrior.

He awakened with a start, thinking it was the middle of the night. But he could see a crack of light out the window, and Mammy was already stoking the stove to make food for them to take.

He thought sure she would be right and the mister would still be asleep or passed out. But he went to the corral, caught the bay and tied it, and then the mule, knowing the mister would be mad if he came out and they weren't ready. He worked hard in the half-light and got both saddles on before he heard the house door open. The mister came out holding a cup of coffee. He had brewed his own, which was unusual because he liked Mammy's coffee better.

He finished the cup, nodded toward Bass, then went back inside and came out with some old blankets and two rifles. He passed the small shooter to Bass. "It's loaded."

Mister tied the old blankets on the mule's packsaddle. When Mammy came and handed him the tow sack of pork and corn bread, she said, "You see that the women are done right and don't make the boy to do it."

It was almost like an order and Bass was surprised to see Mister nod. He said softly, "Don't worry none. I know what you mean."

She handed each of them a piece of corn bread and then stood in the yard watching them ride away in the early light.

The mister rode without speaking, chewing the corn bread, and Bass followed him. It was a little uncomfortable in back of the packsaddle but much better than walking. He didn't know how far they had to ride or where they were going, since he'd never been off the homestead, not even to go to town and help load whiskey or flour barrels. But if it was any distance at all, he would have been exhausted trying to keep up with the long-legged bay on foot. As it was, the mule was wheezing after a couple of miles and now and then broke into a ragged trot to catch up. It was difficult to hang on and make sure none of the sacks or blankets were being loosened and balance the rifle in front of him, all at the same time.

He was surprised that the mister had not brought whiskey but stayed sober and kept the pace up.

In about four hours Bass saw smoke on the horizon, and as they got closer and came up on a rise he saw a homestead ranch a mile away, not unlike the mister's; a scattering of sod or adobe mud huts, some rail corral fence and pens for stock.

But this homestead was on fire, smoke rising out of what remained of the buildings. As they came closer Bass saw that all the stock that hadn't been driven off had been killed. Goats, milk cows, mules and even chickens lay dead with arrows sticking out of them.

The human bodies were hidden in back of the main house.

"Wait here," the mister said. "I'll say when to come." He reached over to the packsaddle and took the blankets, then rode on ahead.

The smell almost gagged Bass; burned hair, feathers, flesh. He took short breaths and tried to hold his head down out of the wind that blew toward him—but still he vomited off to the side of the mule. While he was leaning over, the animal felt the reins loosen and moved forward to catch up to the horse and brought Bass around the corner of the building where he could see . . .

Everything.

The mister had already wrapped one body in a blanket and blood was soaking through it. He was wrapping the body of a young girl. She was naked and there were marks on her that Bass's eyes found against his will before the mister got the blanket around her.

An old man was tied up to the fence rail, held up by the arms. He was naked as well. The old man had been cut many times. There were more than a dozen arrows in him, and there was a fire under him. Bass prayed that the man had been dead by the time the fire had started.

"Start digging graves," the mister said. "Up there, where that cottonwood is, a little south of the tree. The roots will be thicker and hard to dig in on the north side. We need holes as deep as your shoulders. Go. Now. Leave the mule. I'll bring the bodies."

Bass took the pick and shovel and walked up to the tree. He could not stop saying his prayer, and he started crying.

The soil was sandy under the clay and he had a good start on one grave when the mister showed up with the mule. He had made a skid with a couple of fence rails tied up to the packsaddle and a door roped across it. The bodies were laid on the door. He had another shovel he had found near the barn. He started digging as well.

Bass could think of nothing but his prayer and the bodies on the skid. The mister dug intently without speaking or looking up. In two hours they had dug all the graves.

They lowered the bodies into the holes with ropes and then stood for a minute. The mister said nothing, but Bass recited his prayer aloud and then they started filling the graves.

The mister had wrapped them so no part of any body showed as they threw dirt on top of them, but Bass could still not bring himself to drop dirt on their faces. He filled the end where their feet lay and let the mister put dirt on the other end.

The work went faster than the digging, but even so it was getting dark by the time they finished.

"We'll sleep here for the night," the mister said. "We try moving in the dark, and the horses will get snake-bit or step in a hole and break their legs. There's no blankets." He took the horse up near the cottonwood and pulled the saddle and sat down on it in the dirt and leaned against the tree. "Get some of those vittles your ma sent and we'll take a bite."

"You want to sleep here?" Bass asked, handing him the tow sack, knowing he wouldn't sleep a wink this close to the dead bodies. "By the graves?"

For a time the mister said nothing; then he sighed. "Comanches ain't coming back here—there's nothing left for them to bother." He found a piece of corn bread and bit in. "This is the first time they ever come this far east on a raid. I'm hoping it was just the one time and they won't be back." Another bite. He chewed some more. "Garnett is going to hate himself for the rest of his life."

"How come they're like that, wanting to cut and chop people that way?"

The mister shrugged. "They do the same to each other when they fight. I was a Ranger for a time over in the west. . . ." He stopped, remembering. "Where they raided a lot. Time was it wasn't safe to go out to your garden for greens 'cause of the Comanches."

Bass almost shook his head. The mister had been a Ranger? He'd never seen him be anything but fat and lazy and drunk. "But the one that come at me didn't cut me or stick me. . . ."

"He touched you, didn't he?"

"Yes."

"And you had the gun?"

"Yes. But it wasn't loaded."

"He didn't know that. He was showing his courage. To run up and just touch you like that, and he probably yelled an insult at you or told you he wasn't afraid of you, even though you had a gun."

"I was afraid of him."

The mister nodded in the darkness. "I'll bet you were. Now stop talking or we'll be at it all night." He leaned back against the tree and closed his eyes, and soon his breathing became even.

Bass sat in silence for a time, looking at the graves, and thought, Too bad about Garnett and his women and the old man. He meant it to be silent, but somehow it came out loud, and he was startled to hear the mister.

"Any man that brings women into this country should be whipped." Gradually his breathing settled again and he slept.

Bass sat awake for a long time. Had his prayers been enough? Or would the bodies be out wandering tonight because they couldn't get into heaven?

That frightened him almost more than the Comanches, and every time the mule or the horse moved or stamped, Bass would jerk around, looking.

It was a long, long night.

4

FALL 1836

Paris, Texas

In all his twelve years, Bass had known nothing but the homestead. Sometimes people came by and he would hear them talk about the world beyond. Or Mammy would tell him stories of what she called high houses in New Orleans where they had "toney women" with silk dresses and silk skin. She said they were quadroons—women one-quarter black—and octoroons—one-eighth black—and were still slaves even though their skin was as white as clouds and they stayed in fancy apartments on a place called Bourbon Street.

But Bass knew nothing of these places and things except the pictures he made in his head. Wonderful pictures that he sometimes saw in the clouds. But they were imaginary, and he had no real notion of cities or towns or large groups of people.

The town of Paris, Texas, was about twenty miles away, straight east. While the mister went there from time to time, he never took anyone with him. Early one morning a week after they had come back from the Garnetts', Bass was stunned when the mister said:

"Have your ma fix a bag of vittles. Just for you—I'll eat in the saloon. We're going to Paris for supplies and won't be back until tomorrow. Bring a blanket so's you can sleep under the wagon. And leave the shooter here. I can't have people thinking I got slaves that carry guns."

He had not asked for the little rifle back after the trip to the Garnetts' and Bass had not offered it.

"Yes sir. Should I harness the mules?"

"Unless you want to pull the wagon yourself."

Bass went into the quarters for his blanket and a sack of food. Mammy stopped him and made him sit down. "You never been in town before and you got to remember your manners."

"I got good manners. You've been teaching me."

"I mean the other kind, the slave manners. That town will be white people everywhere and you got to remember how to act or you'll get in trouble. Don't walk on the boardwalks."

"What's a boardwalk?"

"It's a plank walk made along the sides of the road for white people to walk on so's they don't get their feet dirty."

"Why can't we walk on it?"

Mammy closed her eyes and sighed. "It's just the way of it. Don't walk on the boardwalks, and if a white man or woman is walking toward you out on the road, you move out of their way. If they talk to you, look at the ground and

40

say 'yes sir' and 'no sir' or 'yes ma'am' or 'no ma'am' and don't ever, ever touch them. The best thing is just stay away from them and only do as you're told."

"But—"

"No buts. The mister never taught you all the rules. Out here you don't need them all. But you're going to town now and I don't want you to get in trouble. Be careful. Mind your town manners."

The last was said to his back as he threw a hurried "yes ma'am" over his shoulder, took the sack and his blanket and ran out to the barn to harness the mules.

He was so excited to be going into town that he could hardly sit still on the wagon seat. The mister drove, the reins held easily in his hands, but the mules seemed to crawl. Bass had never seem them go so slowly and it was lucky he hadn't brought the rifle. He probably would have shot them.

It took six hours from the homestead to the outskirts of Paris. Six hours that seemed like six days, or six weeks, and the only saving grace was that, as they got closer to town where other roads and trails came in, now and then they began to see other wagons and riders.

The mister had let Bass ride up on the seat with him, but as they approached the town he said, "Get in the back of the wagon and sit down." For a second Bass was going to ask why, but then he remembered Mammy's words. He moved back and sat on his rolled-up blanket.

By most standards Paris was a very small town. Eight or ten buildings in a row, five on each side of the center street. The street was plain prairie dirt, and dusty. If it had been raining, it would have been a quagmire of mud.

There were two saloons, a blacksmith's shop next to a

livery, one dry goods store, a square wooden-frame building with a sign that said HOTEL PARIS, and some nondescript small buildings that held a café, a dressmaker's shop, a harness and saddle store and a gunsmith's.

There were people. Everywhere. Bass hadn't thought there were that many people in the world, let alone only twenty miles from the homestead. Wagons rumbled up and down the street, raising clouds of dust, and axles needing grease screeched so loudly it sounded like screaming.

There were stray dogs chasing and biting mules and horses, barking, yapping. Men were yelling at each other and swearing at the dogs and the mules.

One huge freight wagon met them head-on. It was pulled by a span of ten mules, all held in check by one man. His face was covered with hair, his chin whiskers soaked with dribbled tobacco juice. The man swore foully at the mules in a voice so deep and loud it sounded like thunder.

While Bass watched, a horse kicked a stray dog and killed it and two drunk men came boiling out of a saloon, fighting with knives as big as swords. The knives clinked blade to blade, and then one of the men slashed the arm of the other and the fight was over. Blood was everywhere, but the two drunks went back into the saloon.

The mister pulled up in front of the dry goods store and tied the mules to the hitch rail. "Come in with me to load."

The mister climbed down and Bass followed. Just inside the door he had to stop.

The smells were overpowering. Coffee, turpentine, tobacco, produce and many, many smells he couldn't identify because he hadn't smelled them before.

He'd never seen so much of everything in his whole life, or imagined that such a place existed. On a plank counter were glass jars full of the most wonderful-looking things: strips of oily jerky, hard candy in amazing colors, popcorn balls, twisted papers full of taffy. Bass's mouth started to water and he looked away from the jars.

"Here." The mister handed a list to the storekeeper. "Just put the goods on the counter and my boy will take them out. 'Cept the big barrels. We'll roll them up a plank."

Two slabs of smoked bacon almost as tall as Bass were wrapped in paper and he carried them out first. Then bags of coffee and sugar and salt and dry corn for horse feed and a bag of sweet dry corn for cornmeal. The corn weighed almost as much as Bass and he struggled but finally got the sacks up into the wagon. There were many other small sacks with odds and ends, spices and tobacco and the like. By the time they rolled the flour barrel out and up a plank into the back of the wagon, the day was on the edge of dark.

The mister got up in the wagon and drove the mules down to the livery stable, parking the wagon out back. Once there, he and Bass unhooked the mules, took them out of harness and put them in the corral. The livery man— a black man so old and thin Bass thought he looked like a skeleton—fed them grain and fresh hay.

Then the mister took Bass out back to the wagon. "Here." He handed Bass a small paper sack. "Mind you stay with the wagon. You sleep underneath it. I'll be in the saloon playing cards probably till morning. Somebody comes, messes with any of this, you come get me."

"Yes sir."

The mister walked away without looking back, and

Bass looked in the little sack to find it half full of colored hard candies. He hadn't seen the mister buy them and he smiled as he crawled under the wagon and spread his blanket. He had brought the tow sack with food with him and ate a piece of corn bread and some pork and when he was done put just one piece of candy in his mouth.

He had eaten honey and a couple of times rock sugar his mother gave him when he had the croup and kept coughing, but he had never tasted anything as good as that candy. Soon hard dark would come, and he wanted to be able to hold the candies up to the light and look at the brightness coming through the color before he ate them all, but there wasn't enough light and he didn't think he could keep from eating them.

Nearby was the livery barn, and four or five men had a lantern inside and were sitting around on stumps passing a jug and talking. If he tried to listen to them, it might take his mind off the candy.

"Mexico will beat the Texicans," one man said, and Bass wondered who or what were the Texicans. "They got a real army. Sam Houston ain't got nothing but a bunch of scallywags and highbinders."

"Some of them highbinders can shoot you in the eye at two hundred paces."

"Yeah, but Santa Anna has five thousand sets of eyes. That's a lot of shooting when they're shooting back, and them Mexicans got cannon, too. They slaughtered everybody at that Alamo. Took some of them out with that Crockett fellow and shot them in a ditch when they surrendered, and they'll go through the rest of the so-called Texas Army like wet through a goose."

"I dunno. . . . Mexicans didn't want to come up here and fight, and Santa Anna spends a lot of time in his tent with that half-breed girl of his, the yellow rose, so they say. Could be he'd rather do that than fight."

The talk droned on and not a lot of it made much sense to Bass. It didn't matter to him one way or the other who won the war because he'd still be owned by somebody, and the more he thought about that, the more ridiculous it seemed.

How could anybody just up and own somebody else? And why did the law say it was all right for somebody to own a black person who was only one-eighth black—what Mammy called an octoroon—but they couldn't own a white person? And if it was all right to own a black person, why couldn't they own somebody else? Like an Indian? Or maybe a Chinee man, who Mammy said made tea?

Bass snorted and gave a tight little smile in the dark. He'd like to see what would happen if somebody tried to own that Comanche who had slapped him with his sticker. It was horrible what they did to the Garnetts, savage—but a part of him still thrilled to how free the Comanche had seemed on his horse.

Even when he came charging at Bass on that war pony and Bass almost messed his pants, even when he slapped Bass with the side of the spear, he was something to marvel at.

And that made him wonder what if black people had done that, had taken a weapon up and slapped some white man who tried to own them on the side of the head. If enough black men had done that, then the white men wouldn't have been so quick to try and own them.

You hurt somebody, Bass knew from experience, and they quit doing something wrong. Mammy had taught him that when he was a little shaver and played with lucifer stick matches and almost burned the quarters down. She had thumped him good with her knuckles, so hard his ears rang, and he never did it again. He couldn't pick up a match without remembering those knuckles.

He dozed, came awake when he heard movement. Then he realized that the mules in the corral had come over to stand near the wagon to sleep. The sound of their breathing settled his thoughts, and he rolled in his blanket and was soon sound asleep.

⋙⋘

"Come on, dammit, get up!"

Somebody kicked Bass in the backside and he rolled away under the wagon, angry, ready to strike back. It was still dark but just starting false dawn, and it took him a moment to realize that his attacker was the mister, drunk and weaving. "Find a lantern and get the mules harnessed and let's get out of this dump. . . . Bunch of damn sharpers and binders . . . clean a man out of his hard-earned profit . . . full house my a . . ." He broke down into mumbling and fell against the corral fence, hung there for a few seconds, then slumped to the ground half unconscious.

It took Bass fifteen minutes to find a lantern in the half-light of dawn and by that time he didn't need it. He caught the mules with a handful of oats from the livery barrel, strapped their collars on, then hooked the harness around the collars and laid the straps over their backs. In another ten minutes he had them hooked to the wagon and had lifted the wagon tongue to the tongue ring between them and adjusted all the straps, fed the reins back to the wagon seat and then turned to the mister.

He was still down by the fence, half aware of what was happening.

"Got 'em hooked up, sir. Want to get in the wagon?"

The mister didn't seem to hear at first, and Bass repeated himself.

"All hooked up, sir. You ready to go?"

With great effort, the mister pulled himself up on the rails of the corral and wobbled, fell, walked to the back of the wagon, leaned over the open rear end and passed out completely as his face hit the wagon bed next to the flour barrel.

He started to slide out and Bass hurried to catch him. With great effort—the mister was close to three hundred pounds—he heaved the man up into the wagon. Bass threw the mister's old felt hat on top of him, then his own blanket roll, and climbed up into the wagon seat.

Back at the ranch, he had driven the mules to skid logs, so they knew him and settled into the harness when he slapped their rumps with the reins.

The ground was hard, and the wagon rolled easily. Roosters were crowing and dogs barked at the wagon, but little else seemed to be moving in the town. There were horses still tied at hitch rails in front of the saloons, but no other wagons on the road and, except for an old black swamper at a saloon emptying spittoons into the roadway, they were alone.

The mister grumbled and swore but then finally slept, and Bass was alone with the mules and his thoughts. The road led straight west through a treeless plain and it was nearly impossible to get lost since the mules knew the way. Bass was content to let them walk and find their own speed, clucking his tongue and flipping the reins that crossed their rumps now and then to keep their attention.

The dogs barking made him think of the witch-dog coyote that had spoken to him—was the Mexican war what the coyote had been talking about? That might bring a change. Or the Comanche raid on the Garnetts. A terrible change. Or even coming to Paris and seeing a town for the first time, or shooting the rifle and killing a wild pig, or eating hard candy.

That reminded him that he had the paper sack in his blanket under the seat.

There were four pieces left. Two greens, a red and an orange. He took one of the greens and held it up to his eye and looked at the rising sun through the candy. Once he had done the same thing with a green bottle, but this green was much more intense, almost alive, and he smiled at how pretty it was; then he popped the green piece in his mouth, since he had two of them, and looked through the red and then tried to look through the red and the orange, holding one against the other. He was turned backward in the seat because the sun was coming up in the east and he was heading west when he heard a sound in front; he wheeled around and his heart froze.

Off to the side, a small band of mounted Indians was coming out of a gully. In the first instant, the old fear came back, but he saw that something was different about these people.

They were not all mounted. There were five or six men on horses, and walking in back of them were women and children, a dozen or so. None of them were painted and they had no visible lances or bows. The horses weren't painted. Each horse was dragging a pair of skid poles with crosspieces of willow tied in back and bundles wrapped in hide tied on top of the skids.

The horses looked poorly, as did the people. The children especially were very thin, except that their bellies bulged from hunger and many of them, as well as the women, had open sores on their faces and arms. Some held out their hands, begging, and Bass thought briefly of taking some flour and giving it to them. But if the mister awakened while he was doing it, he'd be in trouble, so he looked away.

He hadn't seen them on the road because they had camped in the gully—now he could see smoke from fires they'd put out. After he'd passed, they pulled onto the road going in the same general direction.

The mules were slow, so that the small band almost kept up with him. After another two hours they were still only a quarter mile in back of the wagon and Bass had stopped watching them—they made him sad—and he was looking ahead, thinking if those Indians could be hidden in a gully, then other Indians could be hidden, when he heard the mister wake up.

"Damn rotgut whiskey," the mister said, still slightly drunk although sobering fast. "Had everything in it plus rattlesnake heads . . . who are they?" He had seen the band of Indians back of the wagon.

"I don't know. They came out of a ditch. They're starving hungry and held their hands out for food."

"Creeks," the mister said. "Or Cherokee. Indians from down south. They're moving to the Territory. They might have come all the way from Florida. It's no wonder they're starving. . . . I don't know how they got this far." He fell back against the flour barrel and was soon snoring again.

None of it made much sense to Bass. He didn't know what Florida was, or a territory, but he knew better than to start asking questions when the mister was coming off a bad drunk. And any drunk where he was talking about rattlesnake heads in the whiskey was definitely a bad one.

Besides, the mules sensed that they were getting closer to home. The wagon pulled away from the Indians, and it was a beautiful morning. The green candy still tasted sweet and Bass had saved a red and orange and green to show Mammy when he got home, and he had stories on top of stories to tell her of amazing things he had seen in Paris.

He slapped the reins. "Come on, mules, pick it up. We want to get in before dark."

The mules pretended to speed up, but then settled back into their normal rhythm, hooves clopping in the dust, and Bass sighed.

They would get there when they got there.

5

FALL 1840

Running

Some things had changed.

Bass was sixteen now, pushing seventeen. He was as big as he would be when he became a full-grown man, except that his neck and shoulders had not quite filled. He stood six feet, two inches tall and weighed one hundred and eighty pounds. He could lift more than his weight and throw it in the wagon, and once when a mule had acted up, Bass had grabbed it by the halter, twisted its head and thrown it on the ground.

And if he wasn't quite a man yet in body and mind and knowledge, he had a man's duties.

The mister had battled the jug for three years and had finally surrendered. He would awaken and have coffee, with a little whiskey in it, walk down and look at the corrals without speaking, then go back into his house and drink the day away. Now and then a trip to town for whiskey and supplies.

Bass ran the ranch. He gathered cattle, took care of the stock, shoed horses, doctored sick animals. Mammy cooked and took care of the mister and guided Bass when he needed guidance.

If the mister had been sober, he wouldn't have allowed these things. But as he let go, Bass moved in and began. Like tending the horses' hooves; they started getting too long and cracked and poorly shaped, so Bass took the hoof rasp and fixed them up, evened the bottoms, cleaned the frogs with a hoof pick. Soon the mister left those jobs to Bass entirely.

Or riding after cattle. One day, Bass was rummaging around in a junk pile in the back of the granary and he found an old Mexican *vaquero* saddle with cracked leather and an open seat.

He took the saddle to the quarters and started to repair it. He was surprised when shade covered him and he looked up to see Flowers staring down at him.

"What?" Bass said.

As usual, Flowers didn't speak, but he took the saddle and walked back to where he sat to work.

Three days later he gave Bass what appeared to be a new saddle, oiled, with new stirrup straps and a low-style wrapped Mexican horn. Bass thanked him but Flowers said nothing, just returned to patching a harness.

That day, Bass had put the saddle on one of the mules and ridden him down to the mesquite bottoms, then come back and put the saddle on the Roman nose and ridden him down the same way. When he returned the mister was watching him, standing in the door to his house. But he said nothing, and Bass had been riding ever since, checking cattle, doctoring sick ones, branding the mavericks he caught.

He did not ride the bay, though he wanted to, because he thought of it as the mister's private horse. But he came to like the Roman nose. The horse was smaller, and jerk-gaited, but he was tough and quick, could turn on a dime and was willing to try anything.

One morning, Bass realized he hadn't even seen the mister in two days, and everything that had been done, he had done himself.

On a Saturday near his seventeenth birthday, the mister came to the door of the house and motioned for Bass to come inside.

"It's time you learned how to play poker. Sit at the table."

Bass had only been in the mister's house four times, to help Mammy move furniture. Going inside to play cards was strange, almost spooky. Had the mister gone crazy?

"He's just sick of sitting alone," Mammy told him that evening as they ate. "He don't go to town anymore, but he wants to play a little cards, it ain't going to hurt. Just make sure you lose most of the time."

Bass knew nothing of cards and couldn't read or write numbers or letters, though he could count cattle by fives, and then fives of fives. He had to memorize the face cards and aces and count the spots on the numbered cards. Then he learned the rules, what beat what, and all this took a month, playing two or three times a week with a grubby old deck.

They would play for lucifer stick matches. They played five-card stud, one card down and four up, betting on each

53

card—the mister said it was the only true kind of poker. After the strangeness of the situation had worn off, Bass found that he actually enjoyed it.

Cards came easily to him, especially poker, because he was observant and alert to changes in the mister's manner. After a time he could read the mister's playing.

Soon he had to force himself to lose once in a while, especially when the mister was drunk and sloppy about his cards.

At first the mister was content to play for matches or colored pebbles. But after a couple of months, he wanted to play for something more valuable.

The problem was that Bass owned nothing. Not a thing in the world belonged to him, not his clothes or even his own body, so how could he play for something of value?

So the mister "loaned" him some money to start— twenty-five pennies—and they began playing five-card stud for pennies.

It seemed silly to Bass, who thought of the pennies as no more than lucifer sticks or pebbles, which they kept in a jar in the main house. The pennies remained in two jars, one for him, one for the mister.

Bass didn't think of himself as owning the pennies. He won slightly more than he lost and didn't try to win a lot— as Mammy had advised him—but even so, in a couple of weeks he had nearly forty cents in his jar.

It still would have meant nothing to him, except that the mister decided to harness the mules for one of his rare trips into Paris and take Bass with him. Before leaving, Mister took out twenty-five of Bass's pennies and gave them to him. "Here. You can spend this in town."

Bass was stunned. He knew nothing of money, and he talked to Mammy about it before they left.

"Well, things cost money. Those candies you brought back that time might have cost a penny for five of them."

"So with twenty-five pennies I could buy . . ." He trailed off. The number eluded him, but he knew it was huge. "A whole big bag of them."

"Yes. Or you could buy sugar and cinnamon, and I could make you some sweet cakes to take with you on your cattle-gathering rides."

And that was what Bass had done. He had spent five of the pennies on candy—they were three for a penny—and bought a bag of sugar and some cinnamon. He had sweet cakes when he did the long rides.

And he understood what money meant.

Which made him play harder and win more. That was when the mister increased the limit of their play to a nickel instead of a penny, and soon Bass had more than a dollar in his jar.

He knew a nickel was five pennies, knew it was a great amount of money for him, but did not quite understand how it fit in with the rest of the world. He did not know that a good man could be hired for fifty cents a day, that much of the land in Texas could be bought for twenty and even ten cents an acre or that he was worth eight or nine hundred dollars because he was young and strong. When he was worked out—which happened to many slaves by the age of twenty-five—the rate would drop drastically. Most masters would then sell field hands "down the river," down the Mississippi to the sugarcane plantations in Florida, where they would be worked to death in a year.

He knew only that he had a dollar, which he could use to buy more sugar and spices for cakes. All he had to do was win the money at poker.

So they began playing for a nickel.

And then ten-cent limits.

And then twenty-cent limits.

Bass's jar had more and more money sitting on the shelf in the main house, and he told Mammy that he was getting rich. She shook her head. "You got to be careful, real careful. He's still the mister. It's all his money. And if he gets down on you, it can all go bad."

"I let him win most hands."

"Still, how can you win so much of the time?"

"Just watch his eyes. They get big when he has a good hand and little when he has bad cards. Ain't nothing to it."

"You watch yourself."

"Well, he tells me to play, I got to play, don't I?"

And so they did, once or twice a week for a year, until Bass wasn't sure just exactly how much money he had in the jar, but the mister said it was more than thirty dollars. They were playing for fifty-cent limits by then.

And now, Bass thought, sitting on the Roman nose about a mile from the Comanche crossing, now the mister wanted to bring the limit up to a dollar.

Bass watched as a group of Indians gathered around a wild cow he had tangled the day before. It was caught and cornered on the edge of the mesquite along the stream. They used spears and arrows and the cow died slowly, weaving to jab at them with its horns until it was too weak to fight. One of the braves reached in and cut its throat.

They all jumped in then, women and children, and began cutting the cow open, eating the liver and heart, cutting pieces of meat to eat bleeding and raw. They were starving and wolfed down the meat, not caring that Bass sat less than fifty yards away.

They were not Comanches but had come up from the South like so many he had seen of late, family groups walking. He asked the mister about why the Indians were marching north.

The mister looked up from his cards. "They're Indians from the South, driven out and up into what's being called Indian Territory. North of us. Set aside just for Indians. It's a wild place, full of fugitive Indians and . . ." He looked at Bass and didn't finish.

Bass felt sorry for them, especially the little ones. If they had to go north, they would have to travel where those Comanches had ridden.

That just couldn't be good, unless the Comanches didn't attack other Indians. He remembered burying the Garnetts, and the story of Mr. Garnett when he came back from fighting the Mexicans and found out what had happened. The man had taken a pistol and shot himself up through the mouth. The shot hadn't killed him, but came out his eye and damaged his brain so even when it all healed he looked deformed and couldn't do anything but sit and drool.

Now Bass wheeled the Roman nose away from the Indians; the horse had begun to fidget with the smell of fresh blood. Bass thought he'd rope and drag a cow out of the brush and head home.

He was getting good with the lariat, and he had become a truly excellent rider. The more he rode, the more familiar he became with the horse and its moods. One day, smoke appeared a mile or two away over a rise he couldn't see from the saddle, so without thinking he stood up on the horse while it was walking and studied the smoke. He had been worried about Comanches, though he had seen no more since the raiding party, and didn't realize what he was doing until he was standing on the horse's back as relaxed as if he had been on the ground.

He had ridden barefoot, as he did everything else, until Flowers made him a pair of leather moccasins and a pair of short chaps to keep the brush from tearing him to pieces.

Bass kept his gun with him all the time. He'd tied a leather thong around the grip and the barrel, which he used to tie the gun up under his right leg, muzzle to the rear. Flowers saw this one day and made a scabbard out of softened rawhide so Bass could carry the weapon in front of his right leg.

At first, gathering cattle, he would leave the horse behind, then find and tangle a cow on foot, and go back the next day with a horse to rope it and bring it home. By now the herd was much larger; there were many units of five fives.

But it was slow and dangerous; it was just a matter of time until one of the cattle hooked him. So he worked out a better plan.

He carried a length of rope with a piece of wood across the saddle. The cows weren't afraid of the horse and let him get quite close. Then he'd make a loop, drop it over the cow's horns, throw the log off to the side and run while the cow took off.

He'd come back the next morning, when the cow was tangled in some brush and thirsted out, and rope it and drag it home. Once it was in the herd, usually it would stay around, as long as it had grass and water, and he'd go for another one.

At times he'd have two and even three cows tangled and waiting. Now he'd become a top hand.

While the mister sat and drank, Bass had saved the ranch for him and the mister knew it.

It ate at him.

Now that Bass had started to understand money and knew that the cows were worth up to five dollars apiece, he knew what five dollars was and what it could buy. This made being a slave working for nothing all the worse. There were a lot of five-dollar cows standing out in the prairie around the homestead, and he had brought them all in.

"Ain't nothing we can do about it," Mammy said one night when he was complaining. "White men have the law."

"Then the law is wrong and it should be made right."

"We can talk on it all you want. But it won't change."

He was chewing on all this as he dragged in the last cow of the day. The mister came down to the corral and said: "Poker tonight, after you eat."

Bass didn't want to play, but said, "Yes sir," and finished putting the saddle away and brushing down the Roman nose.

"You suckin' on something sour?" Mammy asked after they had eaten in the quarters. "You look powerful down."

"I'm all right. I'm just tired and the mister wants to play cards."

"Well, let him win some of that money back, and come get some rest. I'll make some Chinee tea and we'll have a late piece of pie."

There would be days, and weeks, and even months when Bass wished he had done exactly that; had just let the mister win.

But he went up to the main house to play in a mood. The mister was playing worse than ever, and Bass won. Even when he tried to lose he won.

First the mister was frustrated at his luck. He couldn't blame Bass because the mister dealt.

Bass had a big pile of money in front of him, and the mister went back to a cupboard to get more money from his tin box. There wasn't any.

"You've got it all, dammit," he said. "How could that be—a darky boy winning all my money? Hell, you can't even read!"

"I'm just lucky," Bass said. "It don't make no mind. Just take it back."

This made the mister even angrier. He took a long pull on the gallon jug on the table, stared at Bass for a full minute and said softly, coldly, "We'll play for you."

Bass didn't understand what he meant, but his voice was chilling. Nothing good could come from this. Bass tried to smile and looked down and said, "Mister, it's all right. We just havin' fun with cards here. Ain't no reason to make it serious."

"I'm dead serious." The voice was cold, flat. "We'll play for you."

"I don't understand."

"I own you. You're worth more than that pile of money in front of you. You play with the money and I'll put you up as stakes. We'll play five hands, winner take all."

"If you win, you get the money. But what happens if I win?"

"You get you."

"I already got me, don't I?"

"No. I own you. If you win, you own yourself. You're free."

And there it was. Freedom.

"You'd do that—set me free?"

"If you win, yes. I keep the money but you go free. But if you lose, I get the money and I still own you." He took another swig.

"What about Mammy?"

"All right. If you win, she can get her freedom too. But you won't win. Now let's play cards. Unless you want to argue all night."

Mammy, Bass thought. Me and Mammy. Free. We would own our own selves. We could go anywhere, be anything we wanted, live how we wanted. We would own our own selves.

"Deal," Bass said, knowing he could win, would win.

He won the first hand.

Then he lost one. The mister had waked up.

But Bass won the third. There it is, he thought. We play five hands. The man who wins three wins the game. I just got to win one more hand, just one more hand, just one more hand.

Then he saw it. The reason he could never win, never be free. The mister had scooped the cards off the table and he had taken them below the edge of the table and left two cards in his lap. Bass had seen the whole thing. The mister was cheating.

Had it been for money, he would have said nothing, done nothing. But this . . . this was for himself. To own himself.

He stood up. "I saw you drop cards in your lap." He reached across the table and picked up the cards. Two aces. The mister would have used them in the next hand and won, and then cheated again, and won again. Bass could see it all slipping away. His heart fell. "You're cheating me."

The mister went crazy with anger.

"Why, you little bastard! You think I cheated you? I'll take a whip to your black hide and show you what manners are! You little whelp." He swung at Bass, caught him a clubbing blow on the side of the head. Without thinking, Bass reacted and hit back, hit back with all the force of one hundred eighty pounds, all the frustration of seventeen years of slavery, all the anger and disappointment of being close to freedom and knowing he would never get it, and the blow drove the mister back from the table and up against a bench by the stove.

Where his revolver lay. He grabbed at the pistol, tried to jerk it free of the holster. Bass knew: I will die. Except there was the jug, the big whiskey jug, and he grabbed it just as the mister cocked the pistol to bring it up to fire. Bass slammed him on the side of the head with the jug so hard, it sounded like he'd broken a melon. There was a loud crack as the mister's finger jerked the trigger, and Bass felt the ball brush past his cheek. Then the mister dropped like dirt on the floor. He didn't move and Bass thought, Oh God, oh God our Father who are up in heaven.

But the mister didn't get up. Bass went to look and thought he could see breathing but wasn't sure and stood there, stood there in shaking agony not knowing what to do, and then the door blew open and Mammy cried, "Oh my Lord, what have you done? I heard the shot. Did you shoot him? Oh my Lord, my Lord . . . I thought he had killed my boy, my baby."

"He tried to shoot me. I hit him with the jug and he missed me."

She kneeled over the mister, put her face close to his. "He ain't dead. Not yet. But he's hurt bad and might die still come morning light. Lot of men with hurt heads die in the first morning light. This is bad, this is so bad."

"He let me play cards for us, Mammy. He said if I won he'd give us our freedom. Then he cheated and I caught him."

She had stood and was watching Bass, studying his eyes closely, sadly. Then she took his face in her hands. "You got to go, my baby. You got to go now."

"No, Mammy. He'll get over this when he comes to."

"No. He won't. You didn't just hurt his head, you hurt his pride. You got to go. Right now. This night, this minute. If he lives he'll be mean mad. He'll whip you and then sell you. Sell you down the river, because nobody wants a slave that fights him. You got to go right now. Go north."

"I can't go without you. He'll be mean on you like he'd be mean on me."

"No he won't. With you gone, me and Flowers is all he'll have to take care of him. He'll yell some, but that's all. . . . But he'll whip you and sell you sure. You got to go, now."

She was pushing him out the door into the dark, pushing with one hand, holding him with the other.

"Saddle that damn Roman nose you like so well and I'll get you some food. Here, take the money." It was scattered all over the floor and she stooped and began gathering it. "You won it, take it. And take his pistol, too. But for God's

63

sake, hurry. If he wakes up, we'll have to kill him sure to keep him off you. Go!"

And without knowing, without really wanting or meaning to, Bass was out the door and running to the barn. He caught the Roman nose, tied him to the rail, found his saddle in the dark and was looking for the saddle blanket when Mammy came with his sleeping blanket in a roll and the little shooter and the mister's own saddle bags. "There's a knife in the roll, and a shirt."

Next to her in the lantern light was Flowers. He handed Bass a beautiful braided horsehair lariat, then touched Bass on the shoulder and said, "You be careful of people you see, and stay off of ridgelines, and don't get the morning light in back of you, and if they set dogs on you, you got to stop and shoot them."

He turned and walked away.

"He talked." Bass was stunned.

"I guess he finally had something to say. Now, ride. Follow the Drinking Gourd north and don't stop until you hear a man call you Mister. . . . Go, my boy, go now or I won't be able to stand it! Oh Lord, my baby . . ."

Bass swung up. Mammy opened the corral gate, and as he rode out, the bay and mules followed him before Mammy could close it. He tried to stop and say goodbye, but she waved the lantern at him. The light unsettled the horses and they moved away before he could tell her how much he loved her, how much he missed her already, how scared he was, how far the place called North seemed to be, how dark it was outside and inside his heart.

He had time only to yell, "Bye, Mammy," and then he was gone into the night, tears streaming down his cheeks.

He cut down in back of the barn to the willows and

mesquite along the bottom, the mules and the bay staying with him, then turned to the right, heading downstream to the Comanche trail.

Then he would head north, north to what the mister had called the Territory.

No mister or master now. Not ever again, because he was like those eagle feathers in the dream. Wild now, wild like the Comanches. They could kill him, but they'd never own him again.

No man would own him.

He was running free, and nothing would make him turn back from that.

Back from freedom.

THE LAND

6

———◆———

1840–1863

The Indian Territory

The place that Bass ran to was known as the Indian Territory. It's called Oklahoma now. Back then it included parts
of Kansas and Arkansas and an edge of northern Texas. It is
filled with people now, and towns and cities and schools,
and churches and hospitals and miles of highways and
roads, and airports and strip malls and hot and cold running water, and forced-air heating and air-conditioning sys-
tems and electricity and streetlights—all the beauty and
some of the ugliness of what we know as civilization.

But a hundred and sixty-five years ago, it was a vastly
different kind of place. So pitch dark at night that people
lived from sunup to sundown, staying close to a modest
campfire once night fell or safely inside the dimly lit cabins
they called home. The stars and the moon were the only il-
lumination on those vast plains once the sun went down.

Even in the long, tragic story that is the history of how the United States government has mishandled its Native American population—some parts seem so horrible they are virtually unprintable—it is hard to fathom how settlers could have stooped as low as they did when the government formed the Indian Territory.

A land-hungry fledgling government attempted to wipe out a people by allowing starvation and disease and hardship to go unchecked. It is frightening to contemplate what might have happened if the American government had possessed the technology for mass extermination of a culture.

The Chickasaw, Creek, Cherokee, Cree and Seminoles—the United States government called them the Five Civilized Tribes of Native Americans—lived in the eastern and southern parts of the country in the early 1800s. The first four tribes were scattered across the southeastern states, with the Seminoles in Florida.

They were by all modern standards truly civilized.

They had towns and settled farms with livestock, and roads between the towns, and farms and written languages and religions (many were Christian), and schools and churches and art. Their culture was in some ways equal to and in many cases better than that of white Americans.

They had spent generations settling their land and cultivating the soil, raising crops that filled complete nutritional needs (corn, beans and squash were unknown to Europeans before they came to the Americas). Since ninety-seven percent of Americans then lived on farms, and since the tribes' farms were successful and, sometimes, large and wealthy . . .

America wanted them.

The U.S. military drove the people off their farms, out of their towns, away from their homes, killing those who refused to go, destroying their culture. Many of the tribes fought to keep their homes, but they could not overcome the might of the American army. The Seminoles fought the hardest, actually defeating the army in a fight called the Battle of Fallen Timbers. They are the only tribe that has to this day never surrendered to the United States government. But in the end, even the Seminoles were driven off their farms and out of Florida.

All these people—men, women and children—had no place to live and seemed condemned to simply wander until they died.

So the United States stipulated a place (the phrase "concentration camp" comes easily to mind) where all the tribes should be forced to go. A wild area was selected that was completely unsettled, one that nobody else would conceivably want, so remote that the problem of what to do with the Five Civilized Tribes would be out of sight, out of mind, and—one would suppose—out of conscience. They called it the Indian Territory.

Unfortunately, it was already occupied by a large tribe called the Osages. The American government sent a small task force to that region, and these officials got two lesser chiefs drunk on cheap whiskey and "bought" the Indian Territory from the Osages for five hundred dollars. The Osages were forced to move—with military "help"—north to a less hospitable region. Many years later, it turned out to contain one of the richest oil deposits in the world. For a brief time, the Osages had the highest per capita income in the world.

The Indian Territory of that time had no roads, no

settlements, no amenities of any kind. The land suffered blazing summers with high humidity, water moccasins, rattlesnakes, copperheads, coral snakes, black widows, tarantulas, scorpions, mosquitoes, chiggers, ticks, very poor soil (compared to the farms back East), countless tornadoes, vicious winters with killing blizzards and ice storms, floods, droughts and poor hunting.

When the Japanese conquered the Philippine Islands during the Second World War, they made the American soldiers who had surrendered march from the peninsula of Bataan to prisoner of war camps. The march was a little over eighty miles long, and more than ten thousand American soldiers died. It is called the Bataan Death March and remembered with horror.

Some of the members of the Five Civilized Tribes had to walk two thousand miles, through wild country, crossing raging, flooded rivers, facing often hostile people and terrible weather. And it must be remembered that what was waiting for them was not the Promised Land—it was worse than the country they had traveled through.

The tribes measured the distance in blood, in bodies. Nobody can even guess how many died or how much they truly suffered. This enforced journey has forever been known by the tribes as the Trail of Tears. It is nothing short of a miracle that any of them made it at all.

It is truly amazing that when they got there they had enough energy and strength left to build camps, settle the country and make homes for themselves. Despite everything, they maintained their compassion and dignity and generosity.

The tribes held together, and their names still live on in the counties where each tribe once lived in Oklahoma.

Other peoples were allowed into the Territory, many of them Native Americans and African Americans running from persecution. Before long, there was a large mixture of cultures and populations. Unfortunately, many people who arrived were white criminals fleeing arrest: murderers, thieves, rapists and con men. The lowest of the low in any culture.

Crime soon got out of hand and the government more or less ignored the whole territory for over half a century.

The Chickasaw tribe started a Native American police force called the White Horse Policemen and tried to instill law and order. For a short time it seemed to help. But in the end the criminal element took control of the entire Territory for almost forty years. Hardened criminals looked on the Territory as their private sanctuary and flocked to the rolling hills and broken gullies that made up most of the land.

Everybody was armed, alcohol in the form of cheap, strong whiskey was everywhere, morals were nonexistent and there was absolutely no law enforcement of any kind. Life was unbelievably cheap. A man could and would be murdered for his watch. A dog or even a child might be shot just to see if a gun was accurate. A woman might be raped because she was in the wrong place at the wrong time.

And into this territory rode seventeen-year-old Bass Reeves.

7

SPRING 1841

Killing Men

That first fall and winter, Bass lived like an animal. He had plenty of money, a good horse, a decent small mule, a good revolver and a good rifle. And all of those things put him in grave danger.

He was a fugitive from the law as a runaway slave, perhaps one who had even killed his master, for Bass had no way of knowing if the mister had died or not. Right or wrong, he had become a lawbreaker, and as a fugitive slave had an automatic price on his head. The amount varied from one to five hundred dollars, but either number was enough to make him a target.

Add to that the fact that he had guns and money and a horse, in a country where a man might die simply because another man wanted his hat. He might as well have worn a target on his back.

He took Flowers's advice to heart and became adept at working below ridgelines, avoiding high places where he could be seen from a distance and staying away from well-traveled trails or tracks. When he had set out, the mules and bay had followed him a good distance, but eventually one mule and the bay headed back to the ranch. Strangely, the second mule—a little female named Bertha—kept up with him. He used Flowers's horsehair lariat to lead her. She didn't have a packsaddle, but Bass had nothing much to carry—Mammy had loaded his bedroll with cornmeal and a pan to cook in, and he had ammunition and powder for both the rifle and the revolver.

Days fed into weeks. He worked his way up through Comanche country without seeing any Indians except the scant few traveling along the trail.

He avoided contact with people, which meant that he rode well off to the side of the trail, and because of that, he saw more game than he would have if he'd been moving where it was better traveled. He managed to kill deer whenever he needed to, and twice in the first year he took buffalo, which stood like cows to be slaughtered. As the first winter began, he also killed some wild longhorns for meat.

The country was rough, broken with stony gullies and little bluffs. When it grew too cold to travel, he picked a short canyon with a rocky back wall and made a crude shelter with downed wood and sod pieces he cut from the dirt with his knife. He left room at the top for smoke to get out and covered the roof with deer hides, used two stiff buffalo hides for a bed, and wintered there, rationing the cornmeal and eating deer and buffalo half raw. He missed Mammy and even Flowers and would have felt sorry for himself except for the knowledge that bad as it was, fugitive that he was, cold as he sometimes got, hungry as he sometimes became . . .

He was free.

Whenever he began to well up with self-pity, he said out loud, "No man owns me or will ever own me again." Sometimes he thought about that witch dog talking to him years ago. "Things will change."

He was living a new life now.

The winter passed without much snow and without his seeing a single other soul. This wasn't strange to him, because he knew that in the wilderness no one traveled much in the winter.

He passed his time tending to the horse and the mule and found them good company; they listened to him make plans for hunting and keeping warm, and the sound of their breathing comforted him throughout the long, dark nights. He spent hours remembering his life back at the mister's ranch with Mammy and Flowers, although he avoided thinking about what might have happened to the mister. He spoke to Mammy as if she could hear him and found it easy and pleasant to imagine her responses. All in all, he was not as lonely as he might have been in his solitary condition.

By spring, the horse and mule looked poorly, all winter having eaten only dry grass they managed to scuff up. But when the grass came green, they seemed to eat twenty-four hours a day, and by the time Bass was ready to leave, they looked healthy enough to ride.

That winter he had made a mental list of things he needed if he could find some kind of a store, and if he dared to head in to buy things: needles and heavy thread, canvas and wool to make clothes. A pair of boots would be wonderful. He'd run off barefoot, and had made a pair of exceptionally crude moccasins out of deer hide and rawhide lacing, which were only slightly better than nothing. In the middle of winter there were times he thought he would lose his toes or feet, and the only thing that saved him was the firewood he found in thick stands of low brush and cottonwood around his camp.

That first spring he worked his way east and slightly north until he started to run into more heavily traveled trails. Most of them seemed to head toward the east and he followed them, until at last he came up on a rise and saw below him, about a mile ahead, what passed for a settlement.

Five small huts arranged in a row along one side of the trail.

He moved back off the rise, tied the mule and horse and watched the settlement for two and a half days. There was a fairly steady stream of travelers going by—some on horse, many on foot—and mostly Indians, although he saw a few who might be white men. It was hard to tell at that distance, though he was fairly certain he had seen some black people too.

They'd stop at the center hut. Bass moved closer and saw that they came out carrying sacks and bundles.

"A store of some kind," he murmured. Just thinking about it made his stomach rumble.

He watched another day and decided he would have to be very careful and try not to attract any attention. He would move the horse and mule back into the brush and leave them. Then he'd take the tow sack Mammy had sent with him and go down on foot, pretending to be a servant or slave sent from a camp by his master to fetch some supplies. He would wait until close to dark, and as soon as he got his goods he would vanish into the darkness and nobody would be able to follow him.

It was a simple plan, and to his surprise it worked perfectly.

He waited until the sun was below the hills. He left most of his money with the horse and mule and took four five-dollar gold pieces—he had learned the denominations while playing poker—and shuffled down onto the trail in what Mammy had once told him was the "darky shuffle," which made whites ignore you. There was no traffic on the trail and he made his way easily, thinking of what he would buy.

It wasn't much of a store, just a shack with some crude shelves filled with sacks and small boxes. He went inside into darkness. When his eyes adjusted, he saw that the proprietor was an Indian wearing a white man's suit, and the second thing he noticed was that, sitting on a barrel in the back corner to the right, another Indian dressed in white men's clothing held a large-bore, double-barrel shotgun aimed dead into the middle of Bass's stomach.

Neither Indian said anything. They sat watching Bass become more and more unnerved.

"I need . . . I need to get some things for Master." He went to the counter and put the twenty dollars in four small five-dollar gold pieces on the rough wood. "Tell me when I spend that."

Neither Indian said anything or moved while Bass went from sack to barrel and back to sack again. There was no candy, which was just as well. He'd been thinking about it all winter and would probably have bought too much and drawn attention.

They sat there and let Bass get a seven-pound slab of bacon. He found some smaller cloth sacks on a shelf and used them to hold twenty pounds of cornmeal, rock sugar and salt. He spied a box of percussion caps that worked for both the rifle and revolver. He felt naked without his firearms, especially when he watched the barrel of that shotgun follow him around. He picked out a cooking pot with a lid, a one-pound tin of black powder and a small block of lead. Both the revolver and the rifle were .36-caliber and he had a small mold and ladle to melt lead.

Each time he put another item on the board counter, he would look at the Indian in the suit and the man would say nothing, so he kept going. Two blankets, a short length of canvas, a twenty-foot length of soft rope, a box of lucifer stick matches, a packet of needles and a roll of heavy thread, and a coarse steel hoof rasp. While there were no boots or shoes, there were knee-high moccasins. He took two pairs down that looked big enough and put them on the counter, and the Indian finally said:

"That's enough."

He nodded, put everything into the tow sack he had brought and staggered out the door.

Outside it was near dark and there was still nobody moving on the trail, although there were some children playing near a hut. He walked a short distance out of the settlement, and when he was sure nobody was following him, turned off the trail and headed into the brush toward his horse, mule and gear.

He was lugging a fair load and it was hard dark. It would have been nearly impossible to find the animals, but they smelled him. The Roman nose whickered to him and he followed the sound.

There was no moon, but at least there were no clouds. He decided against a fire but he could see stars, and he put one blanket on the ground and another on top and rolled them up and slept under the tied horses, luxuriating in the feel of the soft wool, a dead sleep all night.

The next morning he saddled the Roman nose and made a blanket-roll packsaddle, which he put on the mule, to carry what he'd bought. He headed northwest, almost directly away from the trail.

He rode slowly but steadily until he was at least five miles from the trail and had seen no other tracks. There he found a narrow, shallow canyon that went back a mile, with water and good grass coming green, and he set up camp and made a fire. He cooked bacon and made some corn dodgers from cornmeal first soaked in water and salt, then fashioned into patties and fried in bacon grease.

He ate until he was nearly sick, licking his fingers carefully to savor every last morsel and picking the crumbs off his lap. He almost groaned aloud at the delicious taste in his mouth and felt a sudden sharp pang of loneliness for Mammy and her fine cooking.

By then it was midafternoon and he set to work.

He had gone all winter and early spring without a rasp and the animals' hooves looked terrible, with broken edges and cracks. He'd tried to treat them with his knife, and that had gotten him through the winter. Now he tied the animals to a tree and rasped their hooves even and clean with rounded edges.

He wished he had shoes for them, but there had been none in the store, and without a forge to shape them they might not have stayed on long anyway. And besides, anybody who saw his hoofprints now would think he was another Indian; if he had shod hooves somebody might think he had money. Worth following.

He knew little about the Territory as yet, but that shotgun barrel that had followed him around the store told him there must be a serious worry about violence or theft.

In any event, he was a fugitive, and he didn't want anybody thinking he was worth following. For any reason.

He stayed in the canyon for two weeks, cooking on small dry-wood fires that made almost no smoke, eating corn bread and bacon, and venison from a deer he had shot. He was very nervous about the shot, which echoed in the canyon walls. But it was his one shot in the two weeks, and when nobody showed up for two days he assumed nobody had heard it, or if they had, they hadn't thought it was worth investigating.

Being alone with the horse and mule and the animals around him in the trees made him very aware that they could see and hear and sense things that he could not. Through the winter it had not mattered so much. But now the trees were filled with different types of birds, and they sang almost all the time. He learned that if they suddenly grew quiet, it meant that something was moving near them, a coyote or bobcat; when he walked into the trees, they grew quiet then, too.

So he listened and watched the horse and mule, because they could hear and smell better than he could. One morning as he sat on his blanket eating a corn dodger and cold venison from the night before, he looked at the horse and mule, tied nearby, and saw them looking up at the east ridge of the canyon, ears perked forward and nostrils flared to get the scent of something.

At the same time the birds grew quiet.

The hair went up on Bass's neck. It could be a coyote or a bobcat or a cougar. Even a bear or a buffalo. But for some reason this time seemed different. Bass belted his revolver around his waist, took his rifle and stood up.

No sound. Nothing to see.

Then he felt a low drumming of hooves, and, a half mile away, on the low eastern edge of the little canyon, where there was a slope instead of a vertical drop, a buffalo came thundering over the edge and down into the canyon.

He was pursued by two men on horses, one riding on each side. The buffalo came straight at the camp until he was two hundred yards away, then veered and headed out the mouth of the canyon.

The two men saw Bass. They headed for him, firing at him as they rode.

Their shots missed, but one ball passed close enough for him to hear the wind whistle.

Without thinking, he raised his rifle, aimed at the closest man, squeezed the trigger, and saw him throw up his hands and somersault off the back of his horse.

The other man kept coming. He pulled a revolver from his belt and fired at Bass.

Close now, very close, and Bass pulled his revolver, aimed carefully and squeezed. He missed the man but caught the horse in the forehead, and it went head over heels, throwing its rider down so hard, Bass could see the dust thump off his dirty clothes. The horse was killed instantly. Neither man moved.

Bass took half a minute to reload his rifle and put a cap on the nipple—a lesson from the Comanche warrior with the spear—then, careful, walked up to the man who'd been thrown by the dying horse.

He wasn't breathing and his head was twisted sideways at a strange angle. Bass decided the fall had broken his neck. He looked young, not much older than Bass, and seemed to be a white man. He was so dirty it was hard to tell.

Bass walked to the other body. There was a clean hole through the man's chest that must have hit his heart and killed him instantly. He was also fairly young, but an Indian, although he was dressed in wool trousers and a cotton shirt with a wool jacket.

Both of them were almost indescribably dirty, with dirt caked in the folds of their necks and smoke grime on their faces.

Bass stood for a moment wondering that he felt nothing in particular. It had all happened so fast, he'd had no time to feel anything, no time to do anything but react. He stood, wondering what to do next.

This feeling only lasted seconds. Then came an avalanche of thoughts: These men might not be alone, might be part of a larger group sent to chase and kill the buffalo. The rest of the group might be nearby and have heard the shots and might be riding toward him at this moment, and if they caught him in the open, standing, having killed their companions . . .

He had not a second to waste. He looked at their gear and found a double-cinched working saddle in good shape even though it had been slammed on the ground by the dying horse. His own saddle was beginning to fall apart. He stripped the saddle and the blanket off the dead horse and put them on the Roman nose. He strapped his own saddle on the mule to use as a packsaddle. Frantic, he rolled his gear in blankets and tied it on the mule. At any moment, he expected to see riders come thundering down.

The other horse had kept going in the same direction as the buffalo. Gone. Bass was starting to ride away when he looked at the bodies again.

Both men wore boots.

He stood down and ran to the first body, but the boots were too small. He had luck on the second one—they were much larger. He jerked the dead man's boots off and, carrying them as he remounted his horse, he headed out of the valley with the mule in tow, running up and over the west edge, using a gully to get over the canyon wall.

He was tempted to stop on the edge and see if anybody was coming, but uneasiness drove him on. He'd gone five miles and had stopped to let the horse and mule drink at a creek, when he realized he'd made a mistake. Both men had revolvers, rifles, ammunition—and he'd left it all there and only taken an old pair of boots.

Just plain stupid.

"Too late now," he said aloud, feeling the horse jump beneath him with the sudden sound of his voice. "They're gone forever."

He rode up the creek for a mile, hoping the running water would obliterate any tracks, but the mule kept moving off to the soft mud above the water, leaving marks, so it probably wouldn't work.

He thought of stopping, but twice he thought he heard pursuers and kept moving. He was wrong both times, but it didn't matter. He was starting to think of what he had done.

Man killer.

If somebody found the bodies, they wouldn't know he'd shot the men in self-defense. They'd see only the two bodies, unburied, still with their weapons, as if they had been defending themselves, and not the other way around.

He was not only a fugitive slave now but also a man killer.

If there was law out here, its men would hunt him down and not return him to the mister but throw a rope over a tree limb and hang him outright. Mammy had told him what they did to man killers. Hanged them and let the dogs tear at their legs while they died. She had seen it once in New Orleans.

It was bad enough before, thinking he had maybe killed the mister when he cracked him with the jug. Now he was a killer sure, at least as far as the law was concerned.

He had to keep moving.

Wander forever in this godforsaken land.

Like Mammy's Moses on the Mountain, wandering in the wilderness.

Except that he wasn't like Moses.

He had shot men dead.

8

---◆—◆---

FALL 1841

Wolves

Bass felt lost throughout that summer, and he did wander. For two months, he let fear take him, and he never spent more than one night in any camp, often camped cold. When he did make a fire, he kept it very small and dry and would cook enough for three or four days. One meal a day, if a corn dodger and cold meat could be called a meal.

He saw things he did not believe. In his wandering, he ended up back down near the southern edge of the Territory. He didn't know it, but he was getting back into Comanche country.

He lay on a bluff one night, attracted by screams he could not identify as human, horrified to find they were indeed human and that a small party of Comanches below the ridge had captured a freight wagon and were torturing the driver by skinning him alive and burning him in turns.

There were men Bass hated. The mister was in that category. But Bass could not understand torture—the need for it, the desire—and he thought of trying to help the driver. But even if he got one or two Indians, the rest would surely kill him—or worse, do the same to him as to the wagon driver. In the end he moved off the ridge and rode back north, away from the Comanches. But the screams followed him, for weeks, and he could not stop thinking about the Garnett girls and what they must have gone through before death finally released them.

He learned that bluffs were a good place to spend time. He would get on top of them, tie his horse and mule in the middle so they couldn't be seen from below, crawl to the edge, and watch. Often he could see for miles around and remembered that the mister had had a small telescope. He wished he had taken that as well—they could not hang him any higher for adding to his crimes. But even without the telescope, his vision was almost unlimited.

He felt safe, high in the sky on the bluff, and would sometimes find himself looking down on eagles and hawks flying beneath him. He started calling the bluffs by name based on what he saw. One was Torture Bluff, another Eagle Bluff, a third Bather's Bluff, where he saw six or seven children by a homestead jumping around in a pond.

He began to know the country. He found good grass, good water, well-traveled trails and places where people seldom went. He found pockets of game, buffalo, deer and rabbit, where he knew he could find game when his meat ran low.

He came upon scores of small farms and ranches scattered throughout the territory, and would lie overlooking some of them for days, wistfully remembering Mammy and her cooking and love.

He also knew where there were gang hideouts. Usually it would be an older farm or ranch, poorly maintained. Perhaps just a sod hut with a pole corral. There would be few cattle and many horses and men, sometimes a dozen or more.

Even from a distance he could see these were hard men who were always heavily armed, like the two he had killed, and he kept well away from such places, certain that the moment anybody saw him they would begin shooting.

So he kept riding, walking, hiding by night and mostly by day, until weeks turned into months. As he moved, he learned.

Bass was illiterate, and written maps meant little to him. But his inability to read had a benefit. His memory became truly phenomenal. When he saw a special canyon or watering place, or a hideout he needed to avoid, he would kneel in the dirt and draw a picture of the place in the dust, how it looked from above, from the side. He'd look at it for a moment, then erase it.

It was all in his mind now. The Territory was not really that large, perhaps one hundred fifty by two hundred miles, and he covered over seventeen hundred miles that summer, back and forth, up and down, zigzagging to avoid people—and learning, learning, filing everything in a steel-trap memory.

Soon he knew every nook and cranny, every watering hole, every hideout and potential hideout, each of the four "stores," almost every shack or overhanging cave shelter. He felt sure that unless he was taken completely by surprise, it was almost impossible that anybody could capture him. He wasn't cocky, or even overconfident. It was just that he knew all the places he could go to avoid people.

There was no way in the world he could have expected to run into a little girl named Betty.

⟶⋅⟵

Bass had discovered a six-mile trail leading from one small homestead to another. It was about fifteen miles from the well-traveled trail to the store where he'd bought supplies. He decided to visit a different store on his next supply run; the two men he'd killed might have been known at the first store.

He needed to cross the trail that ran between the two ranches and then head north, because in the south there were groups of heavily armed men riding back and forth.

He came to the two homesteads with the trail between them. They were six or seven miles apart, with stands of short brush and woods between them where he could pass without being seen.

Generally, he didn't like to get this close to ranches. There could always be riders out working stock, or somebody returning home.

But to go out and around would add maybe fifteen miles to his journey. He wanted to get north as soon as possible, so he decided to take the risk.

He was cautious. He stopped for over an hour on a rise and studied the trail, looking for movement. Nothing. Then he moved closer, until he was less than a mile from the trail, and did the same thing.

Nothing.

So he decided to make his dash across. No sooner had he started forward at a run than a paint pony came galloping out of the brush on the west side of the trail.

The pony had a little girl riding it and was going hell for leather, well beyond the girl's ability to control it. Bass thought at first that the pony was a runaway—which was bad enough—but as it came closer, he saw it was being chased by three wolves.

When it was less than two hundred yards from Bass, the little girl lost her grip and fell off the back of the pony. The wolves attacked her instantly.

Bass had seen wolves kill buffalo calves and deer. Without thinking, he wheeled the Roman nose and kicked his ribs so hard, the horse blew snot out of his nostrils.

The Roman nose leaped forward into a dead run, but even so, by the time Bass came up to her, the little girl had been bitten on the arms, and two wolves were trying to drag her away.

"Get away!" Bass flew off his horse and into the wolves, kicking at them. "Get away from her!"

One wolf snapped at Bass and ripped his leg down the left thigh, a deep six inches from top to bottom. He didn't feel anything, but he took his Colt out. He killed two of the wolves before the other one ran off, and then he turned to the little girl.

She had several deep bites on her arms and legs that were bleeding, but the wolves had not ripped her face. Bass picked her up as gently as possible and carried her to his horse and swung up. Then he noticed his left leg. Blood poured from the wound, but there was nothing he could do about it now. He rode with the little girl in his arms.

He could not guess her age. Four, five, six, clearly Indian, with long black hair and almond eyes. She looked up at him with a fearless gaze, and though he knew she must be in considerable pain, she was absolutely silent in his arms.

From the way the pony had been running, he figured she had come from the western homestead, so he heeled his horse into a run. Bass looked back once. To his surprise, the little mule was following at a wild gallop.

It would not take long to get to the homestead, and that was good, because Bass was losing blood rapidly. The movement of the horse worked the wound in his thigh, and blood poured down his leg. He had three miles to go, and within a mile he felt dizzy; in another half mile he was faint and hanging on to the saddle horn with one hand while keeping a tight grip on the little girl with the other.

He wasn't going to make it.

He'd never make three miles. He was starting to lose the ability to think straight, and he thought he should stop soon before he fell or dropped the girl. Then everything swam in front of his eyes, and all he could think was he had to hold on, hold on, hold on. . . .

He thought he felt the horse slow—though he kept kicking it to run—and then maybe stop; he thought he heard voices, but they were speaking in some strange tongue and he tried to fight through them; then there was a kind of warm cloud coming down and he thought, This isn't so bad, dying isn't so bad, not so bad at all, and then he was gone.

9

1841–1863

A Family

It could have been hours, days, weeks. He knew nothing but visions and sounds that made no sense. He felt as if his thoughts were swimming in thick water. When he tried to make himself think clearly, he would either pass out or fall asleep.

Images.

A moment of intense pain in his left leg and he saw, or thought he saw, an Indian with black braids leaning over him and putting a red-hot iron onto a wound on his leg, and that made him think of the Comanches and that this must be a Comanche burning his leg, and he screamed and screamed and screamed until he passed into blessed oblivion again.

Later, children's voices, words he did not know, a sing-song sound that pushed him down and down into sleep.

Still later, an old woman feeding him some kind of warm broth, and then, embarrassing even in his dream state, the same old woman holding a jar and helping him relieve himself.

For what seemed an endless time, he simply slept, neither saw nor heard anything; until finally, finally, he opened his eyes, and through the slowly dissipating fog of sleep, he could see where he was.

His last memory was of a running horse. And for some reason, kicking his horse to make it run faster. Then more came: the girl, her paint pony—he could remember the horse's color with surprising vividness—and the wolves, oh yes, the wolves, tearing at the girl.

There were sticks above him, rows of sticks that made no sense. He closed his eyes and opened them again and saw that he wasn't dead and buried, which he had first thought, but that the sticks were willows laid tightly over log rafters. He was looking up at the ceiling of a sod house.

He moved his head sideways and saw that he was in a single room, lying on a sawn-plank bed on what felt like corn shucks. There was a plank table with two benches in the middle of the room, and a cookstove at one end of the room and a low doorway at the other end. Two window openings about two feet square let in light, and from the angle he guessed it was either early morning or late afternoon. All along the wall facing him were plank shelves covered with jars and sacks and cooking utensils. Next to the bed on another bench was a folded set of clothes. With a start, he realized that he was completely naked under a blanket.

He was alone, for which he was grateful, and without thinking he tried to turn and reach for his pants, but he was torn by a ripping pain from his left leg and nearly passed out.

Ahh. He'd forgotten the wolf bite. Taking breaths in short gasps, he gingerly raised the blanket and looked at his leg. There was a bandage over the upper thigh, a wrapping of clean cotton that looked like feed sack material.

He was profoundly thirsty, his mouth so dry he felt as if he had never had a drink of water in his life. On the other side of the bed from the bench there was a jar of liquid on the floor. Carefully, slowly, to avoid turning his leg, he reached down and brought the jar up to his mouth and was overjoyed to find that it held water. He drank and drank, letting the water roll down his throat, until the jar was empty, and just then the little girl he had saved came into the room.

Her arms were bare and he could see scabs healing where the wolves had bitten her. She came up to the edge of the bed, looked at him for a moment, said something he couldn't understand, smiled and then ran from the room yelling at the top of her voice.

Several minutes went by, and then a man came into the room with her. He was an Indian, stocky, wearing trousers and a vest. His hair fell in two long black braids down his back. Bass thought he remembered the braids from a dream about Comanches, but this was clearly not a raiding Comanche, and in fact the man was smiling.

"Peter," he said, coming up to Bass and holding out his hand. "You?"

Bass took the hand. "Bass. Thank you for taking care of me. I would have died sure if . . ."

Peter was shaking his head. "Too fast. No talk good. Talk slow. Again—Bass?"

"Yes. Does anybody speak English here?"

"Me." Peter smiled. "Only one. Rest all talk good Creek."

"Creek?"

"Talk from before. From old places. From home. Speak Creek before come here. Speak Creek here."

Bass was still in a haze. He let his head drop back and sighed. "I'm sorry, I don't understand very well."

Peter nodded. "Bad hole in leg. Take time. Take time. You sleep. We bring food later."

With that, Peter and the little girl turned to leave, but Bass called, "Wait. Peter. What's the girl's name?"

Peter fondly touched the girl's head while he spoke. "White name . . . Betty."

"Betty?"

"White name. Indian name . . ." He thought for a moment. "Be Two Shoes."

"Betty Two Shoes. Thank you. Thank you."

He was alone for a time after they left, lost in his thoughts. His eyes closed and he dozed again, not heavy sleep this time, but comfortable. There was a pain in his leg but it was not severe unless he moved, more a reminder than anything else. The room was pleasant. There were bird sounds outside and warm air coming in the window openings, and he half dreamt, half daydreamed about Mammy and how she would take care of him when he was hurt or had the croup. Memory fed on memory and he realized he'd been gone almost a year. He hoped Mammy was all right, and he remembered how she looked working over the stove making corn bread.

Peter came bustling into the room along with Betty Two Shoes, and two women, one very old, one about

Peter's age, as well as a very old man and a boy of about seven.

They all stood in a row at the foot of the bed looking at him, smiling, standing straight.

Peter said, "This is uncle, named Paul." He pointed to the old man. "And mother, Martha," the old woman; "wife, Mary," the younger woman; "son, Luke," the young boy. Peter's smile widened. "You know Betty."

Bass nodded. "Betty Two Shoes. Later, Indian names for others." He was already patterning his speech like Peter's. "And yours. When I can think good."

They all filed out, except for the old woman. Without showing any expression, she handed Bass a different jar and pointed so that he understood he had to relieve himself. He waited, and finally she laughed a low laugh and turned away, and he used the jar by twisting sideways on the bed. After emptying the jar outside, the old woman came back in and fired up the woodstove. She started frying what looked like boiled potatoes and beef.

When the smell of the food drifted over to the bed, Bass became so hungry he almost growled. She brought him a tin plate heaped with meat and potatoes, and two thick pieces of dark bread spread with bacon grease.

He tried to have manners, but Mammy would have thumped him if she'd seen him wolf down the food, barely chewing it. He ate so fast that the woman had hardly gone back to the stove before he was done and had wiped the plate with the last piece of bread.

"Thank you," he said when she took the plate. "That was . . ." He couldn't think of a word rich enough. "Good. Very good."

She asked him something, then went to the stove, got a cup, and pointed at an old enamel coffeepot.

"Please."

She brought him a cup and he took a sip. It was bitter, but it cut the grease of the food in a good way, so he drank the whole thing.

Then he thanked her again and lay back, closing his eyes, listening to the familiar sounds of somebody working in a kitchen. Homey sounds, gentle sounds.

He had just spent a long winter and most of a year in hard camps where he'd found a certain satisfaction, almost joy, in becoming part of nature so that he could see and hear and smell the world as it was meant to be. Now he was immensely surprised to find that he'd missed home terribly.

He had become a man—standing six feet two inches, pushing 190 pounds—but he found himself acting like a little boy, choking up when he heard the sounds of home.

Martha had her back to him, and he turned his face away to get control of his emotions. When he turned back, she was there, smiling, with another cup of coffee and another piece of the dark bread, this time covered with molasses.

"Thank you," he said, sipping the hot coffee and eating the bread. "Thank you, Ma—" He had nearly said Mammy. "Martha."

But she had turned away and seemed to be making a stew.

His dozing turned to deep sleep again.

The next morning he awakened to the sun and an urgent need to find an outhouse. He was alone. Moving very slowly, he swung his legs ever so gently over the side of the bed and eased his feet down to the floor.

The pain in his thigh was sharp, but not as intense as the day before. Holding to the end of the bed, he stood on his one good leg. He was still naked, and he did not fool himself into thinking he could pull his pants on yet, so he wrapped the blanket around his body. Hopping along the wall, now and then touching his left foot to the floor, he made his way to the door, a simple plank hung on leather hinges. When he pushed it open, he was hit with a blast of sunlight. The heat felt good. He squinted at the brightness and saw a low barn in front of him, made of logs and mud, and a neatly built rail corral that held several horses and mules, his Roman nose and the little mule among them. They looked sleek and well watered.

He saw no people, but off to the left was the outhouse, so he skip-hopped over. If he'd had a cane or crutch, he'd have done all right.

The outhouse was equipped with a sack of corncobs, which was new to him, but he quickly figured out how the corncobs worked.

After hopping back to the house, he was exhausted and lay back down. He wasn't sleepy. It was just that his leg needed rest. He was pleased when Peter came in. Bass's clothes had been next to the bed on a bench, but he had noticed that his revolver and rifle were not there. Peter was carrying them and put them down next to the bed.

"You fought us."

"What? I fought you? When?"

"You . . . riding with Betty. Come very fast. We see wolves and try to take Betty from you. Try to help. You . . .

98

crazy. Call us Comanche. Scream and fight. We take guns. Now all right to have guns. Here."

"I'm sorry. I can't remember any of it. Did I hurt anybody?"

Peter laughed. "Only self . . . swing so hard, fall from horse. We bring you here. I heat iron and close cut."

"I remember that. I thought I was dreaming. . . ."

"You have dream songs. Sang about mother . . . called for her many times. Mammy, Mammy. Sang about fighting man . . . sounds like bad man. Sang about Comanches. Bad. Comanches bad . . . bad for all people. Sometimes Comanches even bad for Comanches."

Bass thought of the Garnett girls. For a time both men sat in silence; then Peter moved the clothes over and sat down on the bench next to Bass's bed. He clearly wanted to say something and was searching for a way to begin.

"Is something wrong?" Bass asked.

"You . . . sing in sleep. Fight song. Dream song. Is all right. But . . . you talk, too. Talk of slave . . . runaway slave. You . . . slave. You . . . run."

Bass was silent. There was not much he could say. There was a price on his head. If they wanted the money, all they had to do was turn him in. He couldn't run now.

Peter touched Bass gently on the shoulder. "We know of slaves. Uncle from South . . . march on Trail of Tears. Saw many slaves in South. Bad."

Bass nodded, still not sure where this was going. "Yes. Bad to own another person."

"You . . . kept Betty from wolves. Hurt self."

"You don't owe me anything for helping Betty."

Peter shook his head, frowning. "Not owe. You . . . save

Betty. Betty . . . now sister. You . . . me . . . brothers . . . family now." Peter cupped his hands as if he was holding a ball. "All one, all same."

"Like I said, you don't have to thank me. You saved me. If you hadn't fixed my leg, I would have bled out."

Peter shook his head. "You, me, Betty, uncle, Mary, Martha. All one."

"Thank you."

"More." Again Peter cupped his hands. "All in here. You want . . . go, you go. All right, good. You stay, stay. Live here. All together. If you want . . . we want."

Bass stared at him, understanding, truly understanding, and knew then that it was what he wanted. A place, a place to be safe, to be with people he could know and care for, a place to be free.

"Please," Peter said. "You stay . . . please. We want . . . please." Peter held out his hand.

"I would like that," Bass said, and he took Peter's hand. "I would like that very much."

THE MAN

10

SUMMER 1875

The Measure of a Man

Bass lived with the Creeks in the Indian Territory for twenty-two years, until 1863. He became fluent in their language. He probably took a common-law wife, although because of the lack of recordkeeping in the Territory, there's no way to know for certain. He wandered now and again, always studying, always learning and always staying well within the Territory, because he was still a fugitive. There was no statute of limitations for an escaped slave. Because the Territory was wild and lawless, nobody would dare to come looking for him.

In 1861, the Civil War started, and in 1863, Abraham Lincoln issued the Emancipation Proclamation, freeing all slaves in the Confederate States.

Now a free man, Bass rode openly out of the Territory and settled into cattle ranching near Van Buren, Arkansas.

His mother was still alive—it is said she outlived him—and she may have come to live with him. He was a very successful stockman and farmer and a true family man. He married a young woman named Nellie, also from Texas, and they raised five boys and five girls. When Nellie died, he married Winnie Sumter and started a second family.

And if that was all we knew of Bass Reeves, it could easily be called an unbelievably full, rich and dramatic life: raised in slavery, escaped and survived the wild Indian Territory, then had two marriages, many children and a successful ranch.

But the legend of Bass Reeves didn't start until he was fifty-one years old. In those days, when the average life span was about forty years, he would have been considered almost ancient, somebody who should sit on a porch and bounce his grandchildren on his knee and watch the world go by.

But in 1875, the lawlessness of the Indian Territory finally came to the attention of the government in Washington. Congress appointed a federal judge who was as tough as the territory he was sent to tame: Isaac Parker. Parker was given the nickname the Hanging Judge because he once hanged six men at once, to save time. He had sweeping powers over the law in the Indian Territory, and his first job was to appoint 200 deputy federal marshals to "clean up" the region.

By modern standards, it's difficult to imagine how immense this problem would prove to be. Parker had to impose order on an area of between fifteen and twenty thousand square miles, with hundreds of thousands of near-perfect hideouts, where the only form of transportation was the horse, and there was no telegraph, no mail service, not even carrier pigeons.

Parker was supposed to bring peace and harmony to this wild place with only a small army of deputy marshals.

And one of the first men he approached was a fifty-one-year-old rancher named Bass Reeves.

Parker knew that Bass had lived in the Territory and was fluent in several Indian languages. He knew that Bass was tough—otherwise, he'd have been dead. He knew that Bass was a successful rancher and hence probably honest, and he may have felt that Bass's being an African American would help, because the people who lived in the Territory were largely Native Americans who no longer trusted the white man. Virtually all the gangs that terrorized the population of the Indian Territory were made up of white men.

The wonder is that Bass, or any of the deputies, accepted the job.

Certainly Bass didn't need to prove anything to himself or to any other man. Nobody could doubt his courage or tenacity. And it's not as if the law had been a particular friend to Bass, who for nearly a quarter of a century had lived in fear of being captured and sent back into slavery.

He certainly didn't do it for the money. Marshals made less than a hundred dollars a month, plus three cents for every mile they traveled if they got the man out alive and if they kept and filed the mileage forms correctly—which, for Bass, who was illiterate, wasn't easy. As with everything else, he did a good job of it. In the end, he collected some fairly large rewards. But he could easily have made money working his ranch and been a lot safer.

There is a legend about the Texas Rangers. In the West, salt was the only way to preserve meat. It was a vital commodity and had been free until an El Paso man "claimed" a salt bed near town. He tried to charge for it and caused salt riots. The good people of El Paso sent to the Rangers for help, and the Rangers sent one man. The saying was "One riot, one Ranger," because they were so tough. Now, if this legendary incident happened at all (it's not documented), it only happened once.

But Bass Reeves was forced to show up alone all the time. Parker, or one of his assistants, would give Bass a stack of warrants or subpoenas for half a dozen or more killers, rapists, molesters, thieves, man burners—the worst kinds of outlaws, and not just one or two, but whole gangs of them—and Bass was supposed to saddle his horse and collect his weapons. He carried as many as four revolvers, two rifles and a shotgun at times. He'd ride alone into what many men called the center of hell and bring the men out—alive, if possible, or, if necessary, draped dead over a horse.

He did this three thousand times.

During the Second World War, the bomber groups bombing Germany had a cap of twenty-five missions, because the Air Force realized that men needed to see an end to the danger to be able to risk their lives daily.

Bass had no such cap, and he must have known that the odds against him were absolutely staggering.

And yet he never shied away from an assignment.

Nobody ever sat down and interviewed Bass as they did with Hickok, Earp or Cody. Racial prejudice—another enormous obstacle for Bass—may have been at its worst during the years when he was a marshal, right after the

Civil War, when millions of African Americans were attempting to live free in a racist, bigoted nation.

So there is no documented explanation of why Bass Reeves would accept the offer from Parker.

But even if it's not documented, there's still a logical reason for Bass's taking the job and the huge risk it entailed. Bass had lived in the Territory with the Creeks for just under a quarter of a century and was accepted by their families; was sheltered and hidden by them; loved and was loved by the very people who were now being victimized by these criminals.

Perhaps he thought he owed them some kind of help.

Whatever the reason, in the summer of 1875, Bass Reeves put on the badge.

11

1875-1909

True Grit

Bass lay beneath some brush and watched the cabin a half mile away in the approaching twilight. It was back in a cut in the Cherokee Hills.

It was starting to rain. He was grateful for the rain because he was disguised as a bum just looking for food, and the worse his clothes looked, the better. His good horse, a red stallion with a white blaze, was tied a mile and a half back in a stand of thick aspen where he wouldn't be found. Bass was riding an old mule that he'd brought with him as part of his disguise.

The day before, he had crossed the dead line, a line eighty miles west of Fort Smith, Arkansas. Most deputy marshals didn't cross it, and those who did were almost always killed.

For the past thirty miles, he'd been in extremely dangerous territory. He was glad to look like a bum who didn't have anything worth stealing.

It gave Bass a deep thrill each time he crossed the dead line.

Like pulling a lion's beard. Bass scratched his cheek. Three weeks earlier, on a short run that ended in a wild gun battle, he'd disguised himself as a woman. He'd had to shave off his handlebar mustache and had worn a big sunbonnet and a full-skirted gingham dress. He'd gone into the camp of a gang of horse thieves and killers, pretending to be an old lady who was a friend of a gang member's mother. Bass had expected just three or four outlaws, but there were over a dozen. He still thought he might be able to pull it off and get the two men he was after by waiting until the others rode away. But one of the outlaws noticed that Bass ". . . is the ugliest woman I've ever seen, and she has a beard showing." Somebody in the cabin wanted proof he was a woman, and when he pulled a gun instead and told the men they were under arrest and to ". . . surrender peaceful-like," somebody yelled, "Hell, he ain't nothing but an old lady," and started firing. They shot holes in his dress, shot his bonnet brim off, cut his gun belt under his dress and shot a boot heel off before he gained control of the situation by killing two of them and wounding two others.

Bass smiled now, remembering the look on Judge Parker's face when he'd come riding into Fort Smith with ten live prisoners tied together in tow and two dead draped over their horses. When the wounded men had complained about being tied together, he'd just said, "It's easier to carry you dead." When they looked at the bodies of their companions, they quieted down.

Parker had called him "my bargain-basement deputy," saying he "brings them in cheaper by the dozen."

Now Bass narrowed his eyes. The door of the cabin opened and a man came out and relieved himself off to the side. It looked like Dozier, but at this distance he couldn't be sure. He had been hunting Bob Dozier, who was wanted for horse thievery and for killing the drovers who had the horses, for almost three years now. Bass had come close to catching him, but the man was slippery. But Bass knew for certain this time that there were only three men in the cabin.

Everything was going well, he thought, glad of his disguise but sick of lying in the mud. Man wasn't supposed to lie in mud. It wasn't natural. He eased the Colt .38–40 into a more protected position under his clothes. Normally he carried two of them, with butts facing forward for a faster draw and more safety when riding in thick brush. That brush could snag on the hammer, cock the piece and discharge it down into the horse. This had happened to many a cowboy chasing wild cows.

Bass also had a Winchester lever-action rifle chambered for the same round, .38–40, so he usually had to carry only one kind of ammunition.

But he had left the rifle and his other pistol and gun belt with the stallion. No bum would have a weapon, and if this was going to work at all, he had to play the part well.

He felt a night chill coming on. It was summer, but the rain had soaked him and a faint breeze blew. He stood slowly and went back to the mule. He had an old saddle on it, all part of this disguise, which he used fairly often. He also posed as a drover, a cowboy, a dirt farmer and an outlaw. Anything to get close enough. You had to get so close you could smell their breath. . . .

He mounted the mule and forced himself to slouch. Normally he sat straight up on the stallion—he was a master horseman—but an old drunken bum would hang over the mule like the old clothes he wore. He had even taken the heels off a pair of boots so he would walk in a shambling, drunken gait.

Half a mile to the cabin. It was dark enough now so that a lantern shone through an oiled-paper window. He knew they wouldn't be able to see him coming in the rain with the dark hills in back of him. With the mule walking in mud, they probably wouldn't even hear his hooves on the ground.

Bass rode up to the cabin door without being discovered. He sat for a moment, preparing. When there was time—there wasn't always—he would compose himself and try to anticipate how things might go. There were three men, all potentially dangerous. He had a warrant for Dozier and a couple of John Doe warrants if he needed them. He would knock on the door, pretend to be begging for food, take it from there.

He stood down from the mule, adjusted his revolver under his coat so he could get it in a hurry. Then he knocked on the door. The talk inside stopped instantly and he heard stools or chairs scraping as people got up, footsteps, a moment's hesitation; then the door opened a crack and a gun barrel poked out.

"Sorry, boss, don't mean no trouble. Just looking for some work to make some food." Bass moved back to appear less threatening. "Mighty hungry, boss. Eat just about anything."

The door opened wider and a face appeared. Not Dozier. White man, mid-twenties. Stood looking at Bass in the dim lantern light, then turned back into the room. "Hell, Bob. It's just some old nigger begging for food. We could let him peel the pota—"

"Old nigger, hell—that's Reeves!"

Bass knocked the barrel of the young man's revolver up in the air and threw his shoulder against the door, jamming it in against the man, knocking him to the floor sprawling, the gun flying out of his hand. Bass drew his Colt as he came in.

But at the same time, there was the sound of a door slamming open on the other side of the house. Most hideouts had an escape door in the back, and Dozier had gone out as Bass came in.

Bass kicked the gun away from the man on the floor. A second man stood by a cookstove, holding a frying pan, his mouth open.

"Your gun," Bass said, pointing at the man's belt and holster. "Out now. Two fingers. Throw it over here. . . . Do it wrong and I'll kill you. I ain't got papers on either one of you, so don't push the hand. Both of you leave your weapons and run outside and just keep running north, and I'll let you go this time. Don't come back or I'll kill you. Do you believe me?"

"Are you Bass Reeves?" The man by the stove had thrown his gun away, onto the floor.

"Yes."

"Then I believe you."

"Get."

"Horses?"

"No. On foot. Go now before I put one in you for luck."

Both men jumped to the door and vanished in the rain and dark. Bass went to the back door. He thought Bob might make for the corral, just east of the house; he might try to get to a horse and ride. But Bass was wrong. There hadn't been enough time, and Dozier had elected to stay and fight. As Bass came to the door, he hesitated, peered around the door frame and for his foolishness was rewarded by a splinter of wood chips in his eyes, as Dozier fired and missed his head by not more than three inches.

Bass went out the front door and then worked around the west end of the cabin. He stopped at the corner. The rain was coming hard, but he was sure he heard footsteps running away to the south. He jumped around the corner and ran after them.

Stupid, he thought. Chasing after him in the dark. But he kept going, and this time his luck held. He saw Dozier trying to run, ahead of him. The mud was ankle deep, and as slow as Dozier was going, Bass could barely keep up. The range was terrible for a handgun in the dark, a good forty yards, but he stopped and squeezed off a round.

Shot wide. To the right. But the sound of the shot made Dozier stop and turn, and he fired twice at Bass. Missed. Bass had kept moving and had closed the distance to thirty yards.

Bass stopped, aimed more carefully and fired again. Dozier jerked in a half spin to the right and then straightened up. His gun arm hung down, but he reached across with his left hand and took the gun from his useless right one, started to bring it up.

"Don't, Bob." Bass wasn't twenty yards away. "Don't do it."

"I ain't going to let that son of a bitch Parker jerk my neck for all them damn farmers to see me piss my pants."

"You might get prison." Bass knew better. Dozier had murdered two men in cold blood. Parker would hang him as soon as he was found guilty.

Dozier had the gun in his left hand and was awkwardly trying to cock the hammer, wobbling the Colt around.

"Don't, Bob."

Bass cocked his own Colt, aimed carefully at the center of Dozier's body, and when the barrel of Dozier's Colt started to come up to point at him, Bass squeezed the trigger.

In the flash from his revolver, he saw the big slug take Dozier high in the chest, but the man still stood. Bass thought, All right, double tap, and shot him again in the forehead. Dozier went over backward and Bass walked up to him. He automatically ejected the spent shells from his Colt, a habit he'd kept all these years after the Comanche had charged him and he had an unloaded rifle. He reached around for new cartridges from his belt before he remembered that he had left his gun belt with the stallion.

He looked down at the dead man. He'd been chasing Dozier for three years. He felt almost nothing and did not know why. There wasn't much light, but he saw the hole in Dozier's head and noted that it was a little high and thought, Oh yes, I always shoot high at night. Just a little. I'll have to watch that. . . .

Then he started shaking, and he didn't know if it was from the chill of the rain or from the killing.

Even when it was necessary—and he'd had no choice

at all with Dozier, and knew it in his heart—he did not like killing. It was such a waste.

Two drovers dead and their horses stolen.

Dozier lying faceup in the mud, rain pouring into his unblinking eyes. Some mother must have loved him, must have suckled him, must have fed him and changed his diapers. . . .

Just a waste of everybody.

❧⸙❦

Some were quick.

Tom Story was that. Another killer and horse thief with a set of relay ranches—shacks in the woods—who had killed drovers and stolen horses and sold them down across the Red River for years before Bass went after him.

Bass did the usual preparation. Checked his guns. Had somebody read the warrants to him so he knew which one was Story's. Rode his stallion wearing his good black hat with the flat brim turned up in the front so he could sight his rifle, wore his good riding suit, had his boots shined in Fort Smith before he left but took his mule and old clothes in case he needed to go in disguise.

Did it all right and proper, figured on being gone at least two weeks, and then came around a corner and met Tom Story driving a herd of stolen horses across the river at the Delaware Bend crossing. Came riding right up on him, out of some brush, the two of them mounted and not twenty yards distant.

Two seconds of surprise on both parts.

Tom jerked first. "Fill your hand, damn you!" he yelled, and he fired wide to the right while Bass was drawing his left Colt with his right hand, easing the hammer back as he pulled it from the holster, raising it while Story shot a second time and cut the right rein so close to Bass's fingers, he felt a breeze from the bullet.

Bass had his weapon up by this time and he aimed, squeezed and hit Story about a foot above the belt buckle. Story bent forward as if he'd been kicked in the stomach by a mule, and it was finished—except that he still held that gun, so Bass cocked and fired again, taking him in the temple. Then it was truly over.

Story's horse wheeled and carried the body some twenty yards before it fell off. Bass reloaded and thought, One day out, one day back.

I didn't even get to the dead line.

⇥⊷ ⊶⇤

Some were hard.

Horses were vital to people's welfare back then. There were no cars, and trains did not come to that many towns, so horses were for riding, working, pulling, hauling— every kind of work. Stealing horses then was like stealing cars now. They were in huge demand, there were never enough of them, and there was always a ready market.

Jim Webb, a horse thief and a cold-blooded killer who actually carved notches in the wooden handle of his Colt for every man he killed—eleven—was very nearly fatal for Bass.

Bass tracked, hunted and hounded Webb for more than two years. Like Dozier and many other thieves, Webb had a series of relay stations. Relay ranches were very much like chop shops are for cars now. A stolen car is taken into a chop shop and either has its appearance radically altered and is resold or is cut up for parts. A stolen horse was taken to a relay ranch, where its brand was altered and allowed to heal, and then it was moved through a series of relays until it was far enough from its home not to be recognized. Then it was sold. One horse might be worth forty dollars—a full month's pay for a hardworking man. Horse thieves ran a big, lucrative business.

Webb stole horses up into Kansas, over into Arkansas, relayed them through the Indian Territory, then down south across the Red River into Texas, where they were sold to the military or to ranchers and farmers.

If a man had a horse, or a ranch had a dozen of them, and Webb wanted them, he simply frightened the owners enough to let him ride off with the stock, and if that didn't work, he murdered them. He was absolutely without mercy, and Bass was determined to get him.

Webb knew that Bass was after him, and he kept changing relay stations and methods, always staying one jump ahead, until finally Bass decided to forgo all other warrants until he got this one man.

Following rumors, hints, guesses and hunches, he worked across the dead line in late 1894 and came to a stream of prints from at least twenty horses. He was riding the stallion. This time, for disguise, he brought two geldings, both longlegged and tough, excellent long-distance runners. Webb was known for running long with spare mounts to get away, and Bass was planning to stay with him. But at the moment things weren't going right. Bass had cornered a notorious small-time thief named Charley One-Finger—he'd been born with only one finger on his left hand—near Shepherd's Crossing. Bass threatened him with a John Doe warrant, "just for being a bad influence," if Charley didn't tell him where Webb was hiding. Charley lived in fear of coming up before Isaac Parker, and in his terror told Bass that Webb was going to run a big herd of stolen horses down into Texas soon. "Maybe he's doing it right now. Maybe you better go look."

Now Bass studied the prints. This was an older set of tracks, a cold trail. The edges of the hoofprints looked weathered and had been blown round. There had been no rain and no wind for at least three days, so the tracks were at least that old. Probably more like a week.

Could be Webb, Bass thought, and then shook his head. Wishful thinking. Could be anybody. Still, somebody with a herd of more than twenty horses heading southeast was more than likely up to no good.

So he brought the stallion and the two geldings around on the trail and started to follow it. It was a beautiful day for a ride, even if he had crossed the dead line and had to watch every ridge and stand of trees for potential danger. The sun was coming up to noon and the warmth felt good on his shoulders, eased a small ache that was starting to visit him on a cold morning. He'd ridden thousands of miles on hundreds of horses and been thrown by a few, and he supposed the new ache was a memory pain from getting thrown on his head and neck more times than he wanted to count.

He was seventy.

In his work and life, in his thoughts, in his dreams at night, he was still in his twenties, but seventy summers had passed and here he was, the stallion under him, his Winchester scabbarded under his right leg, two Colts at his waist, a double-barreled shotgun hanging by a leather loop from his saddle horn, a pocket full of corn dodgers (he still liked them for trail food) and a full canteen of water. Still riding, still hunting.

"What the . . ."

The stallion had stopped and fidgeted as if there was a mare in season nearby. Bass studied the ground and saw that another group of horses had come into the older trail from the north. Ten or twelve, it was hard to tell unless he got down and memorized the different tracks so he could identify and count them.

No matter the count, the tracks were dead fresh. One must be a mare the stallion could still smell. The soil, where hooves had cut the earth and thrown it up, was still damp-looking. And the sun was baking straight down.

Not days, just hours, ahead of him. Maybe three hours.

It was Webb.

He didn't know why he felt so certain. God knew over the past two years he'd been close before, but never close at the right time. Either he only had the mule and couldn't get into a long chase, or he was escorting prisoners back to Fort Smith. There was always something.

But this time it felt right. This time, this time . . .

He heeled the stallion into a faster pace, an easy trot. They would be walking the horses, and if they were three hours ahead, that couldn't be more than ten or twelve miles. If he trotted, he'd be doing six to their three or four. In five hours he'd be up with them.

He had no plan as to how to handle Webb and the herd. With hoofprints this numerous, he couldn't tell how many riders Webb had with him. Three could handle a herd this size, but there could be many more.

Ideally he would catch up to them without being seen, wait his chance to get the drop on Webb. He had no illusions about Webb's surrendering if there was the slightest chance he could fight his way free. Webb would run if he could, but if he couldn't run, he'd try to kill Bass.

In any case, it was taken out of Bass's hands when he was still two miles from the herd.

He knew they were close. The stallion had a mile-eating trot, and the two geldings had no trouble keeping up. Bass stopped to study the trail, felt a pile of fresh manure with the back of his hand. Still warm. He remounted and hadn't gone another half mile when he saw something ahead.

As he got closer, he saw it was an old boot top, cut off and sewed into a long pouch. This was the way many rustlers and thieves carried spare cartridges. He leaned down and picked it up without dismounting and saw it had fifty or sixty .44–40 cartridges inside, no good to him with his .38–40 handguns and rifle, but he dropped it into his saddlebag and had just faced front when a man came loping around the bend ahead of him, looking for his lost ammunition.

The man was so surprised, he didn't stop his horse for another thirty or forty yards. He was still more than a hundred yards away, but Bass pulled his rifle.

The man hauled on his horse so hard, it almost went over backward. He wheeled and dug in his spurs. Bass could hear his horse grunt in pain even from a hundred yards away. The man wasn't Webb, but Bass spurred the stallion into a run to keep up. Running loose, the stallion could have caught the man easily, but pulling the two geldings slowed him a bit. Bass didn't want to let the geldings go, thinking he would need them if a chase developed.

He didn't try to catch the rider, but held pace with him as they rounded the bend and he saw the herd of horses about a mile and a half distant. There were two riders. The man running in front of him yelled, and when the two riders still didn't see him, the man pulled his pistol and shot in the air.

They both wheeled. The rider on the left just sat looking, but the one on the right spurred his horse and started north up a gully that led to the top of a flat plain that had no visible end. He was pulling two horses running bare in back of him, as Bass was, and Bass nodded.

Webb. That would be Webb.

It would be a chase. For a second, Bass was surprised that Webb headed onto a flat prairie to run north, where there would be no place to hide, but then he realized it was the right move. Webb had no choice. If he tried to run around the herd and head west or south, it would take too long and Bass might come within range for a shot. Bass was accurate—no one would let him compete in turkey shoots because he always won—and everybody in the Territory knew it. Especially criminals.

Webb was moving faster than Bass was, but Bass made no attempt to increase the stallion's speed. The big stud was the best horse Bass had ever owned, but he had been ridden all morning and Webb had probably been changing his mounts from the herd he was pushing. Still, the stallion's long legs would keep them in sight.

There would be plenty of time to close the gap. The

way Webb was running, he'd blow the first horse out in half an hour, just when the stallion would start to slow. Then they'd both be into their remounts, and if Webb kept up the pace, the remounts would last no more than a half hour each. That made the chase, at the most, another hour and a half.

Twenty-two miles. Maybe. Not more than twenty-five or twenty-seven. Bass took a quick look back as the stallion barreled up the gully and onto the flats, the geldings scrambling to keep up. The other two men were running south, and the damn fools were taking the horse herd with them, which would slow them down too much to get away if Bass came back after them. In any event, they weren't coming after him to help Webb—loyalty was a scarce commodity with the gangs. Knowing this had saved his life hundreds of times. If gangs had ever worked together, he'd have been dead by now.

The stallion tripped on a soft gopher mound and Bass held his head up, felt him through his legs to see if he was weaving, getting tired, but he was still moving well. It was just a momentary stumble. Still slightly slower than Webb, but the speed was evening out.

What was twenty, thirty miles ahead? Bass had wandered up there when he was a fugitive two or three times. He hadn't liked to get too far north because some of the tribes up there were as hostile as the Comanches.

All the way up into Kansas, if his memory was accurate, were rolling, shallow hills—undulations in the prairie. Which was good. He needed the hills if the chase got long, to close the distance, assuming all the horses were about equal.

The stallion had seen Webb's horses ahead of him now and knew they were in a chase. He had done this many times. Bass let him pick his own speed and was gratified to see he was gaining just a little.

Bass checked his gear for the third or fourth time, pulled his canteen up and took a sip, rolling easy with the stallion, looked back to make sure the geldings were moving well.

Twenty minutes passed, and he was only a mile back now. But the stallion was pulling longer breaths, and Bass knew he would have to change mounts soon. Ten, fifteen more minutes, and he would be starting to drop back if Webb held the same speed.

Fifteen minutes, and the stallion told Bass it was time by starting a slight weave. He was getting tired. Bass didn't want to blow the horse out, so when the weave became pronounced, he pulled the big animal to a stop, unfastening the cinch as he dismounted. He drew the blanket out from beneath the loosened saddle, slapped it on the first gelding, then threw the saddle, rifle scabbard and bags over on the blanket, tightened the cinch, pulled the bridle off the stallion, buckled it on the gelding. He was remounted and moving inside a minute and a half. The stallion followed willingly, glad to have Bass's weight off his back.

As soon as Bass had stopped, Webb had stopped too and changed mounts. He was slightly faster and gained a bit, but Bass wasn't worried yet. As long as he held his own through the second horse, it didn't matter if Webb was under the impression that he'd moved further away from Bass. Bass would make his move on the third horse. The plan was based on a thorough knowledge of horses and how they ran. Like people, horses used more energy and did more damage to their muscles and joints running downhill than they did uphill—even a shallow downslope would jar their shoulders and back and quickly cause powerful fatigue.

Years ago, an old and peaceable Comanche had come to visit the Creek family and told Bass how he was able to outrun Texas Rangers, even when the Rangers had better mounts.

"As soon as they can't see you, get off and run downhill. Then, before they see you again, get on and ride. They think you ride all the time. They ride the whole time. You only ride uphill and flat. Pretty soon their horses stop. Your horse keeps running."

Bass had used the method many times to catch fugitives. He even had a pair of flat-heeled boots for better running. Most of the men wore high heels to keep their feet from slipping through the stirrups, which could mean getting dragged to death. Bass had told nobody of his method, not even other deputies, for fear that it would be used by the outlaws. So far none of them seemed to know about it.

An hour passed, and Bass's gelding ran easy. The stallion knew what would happen and stayed grazing where Bass had left him. They were almost exactly even in speed. Webb would gain a little, then Bass would gain it back.

At the end of the second half hour, the gelding started blowing and made a slight weave. Bass quickly stopped him, hoping Webb would do the same. Again, Webb was a little faster changing the saddle than Bass. But soon they were both moving again, still about a mile apart, both horses running easily the first fifteen minutes.

Bass took his feet out of the stirrups and shook his legs to loosen them. As the gelding started down a shallow slope, they dropped out of Webb's sight, and Bass quickly dismounted and ran easily down to the bottom, not fast but steady, perhaps only two hundred yards. Then he re-mounted, and as he came up the rise, he saw that Webb had gained almost a hundred yards.

Webb saw it as well, and his reaction pleased Bass. Webb probably thought Bass's horse was blown, and he pushed his mount harder, trying to gain enough to get out of sight—but at great expense.

Meantime, whenever Webb was out of sight, moving down, Bass got off and ran. His horse actually seemed to find energy and stamina and soon Bass started to close in on Webb dramatically. Webb whipped his horse harder.

Three quarters of a mile, then half a mile separated them, and Webb knew he'd been duped. His horse was weaving and staggering.

It was all over.

Webb stopped his horse, turned him, pulled his rifle from the scabbard, wrapped his reins on the saddle horn and spurred his horse straight at Bass, firing as he came.

It was a brave, stupid thing to do, Bass thought, pulling his own rifle from the scabbard. Webb should have got off and found cover, fought it out. Bass heard Webb's bullets going past, but they were wild. One came close enough to make the telltale crack in his ear, which meant it was only inches away. That was close enough. When they were four hundred yards apart, Bass pulled the gelding to a stop, stepped down in back of him and, aiming over the horse's back, squeezed the trigger. He watched the bullet take Webb off his horse backward.

Webb lay still. His horse moved off fifteen or twenty yards and then stood, sucking air.

Bass remounted, used his knees to steer the gelding up to where Webb lay, aiming his rifle at him the whole way. He had learned long ago never to trust a downed man, and Webb was still moving, his legs shoving his feet into the dirt.

Bass stopped fifteen yards away. "Can you hear me?"

"Yeah." Webb's voice was muffled and he fought to turn over on his side. He propped up on one elbow, then sat up. "You gut-shot me."

Bass saw the deep red blood staining the front of Webb's shirt. He saw Webb's rifle ten yards off to the side where it had flown when he went down, and saw that his sidearm holster was empty as well, the Colt knocked clear when he hit the dirt. Webb might still have a hideout gun, but he would have to move fast to get it and Webb, Bass knew, was done moving fast.

Webb squinted up at Bass. He had dirt in his hair, in his eyes, all over his face. The evening sun seemed to give him a ghostly pallor. "How'd you catch me?"

"I ran downhill, rode up. My horse rested on the downhills, yours kept working. Learned it from a Comanche."

"Damn Comanches . . ." Webb trailed off, grunting. The shock of the wound had kept the pain away for a few moments; now it came. "God . . . this hurts. How long do you think I've got?"

Bass knew what the dark blood meant. Webb's liver had been hit. Gut-shot men with whole livers could live days, the pain so harsh it almost destroyed their minds. With the liver hit, it wouldn't be an hour. Webb would bleed out inside. But Bass said nothing. Webb would learn soon enough.

"You're tough, Reeves." Webb grunted the words slowly and painfully. "I want you . . . to have my scabbard . . . rifle. Take 'em."

Bass nodded. "Is there anybody to tell? You got kin?"

Webb tried to laugh but only winced. "None that want to claim me."

He fell silent, eyes closed, leaning precariously on one elbow. Bass thought he was dying, but then his eyes opened and he smiled. "Would you tell the truth . . . to a dying man?"

"I might."

"They say you shot Billy Leach . . . for throwing . . . hot bacon grease . . . on your dog. . . . That he fell in the fire . . . you let him burn?"

Bass sighed, remembering. He had been in disguise, pretending to be a horse thief, sitting with a gang cooking bacon. He had his hound with him, a dog he was very fond of and that he'd had a long time, and Billy had thrown hot bacon grease on the dog's head just to hear it scream. Later, the court let Bass go, saying he was cleaning his rifle and that it went off by mistake.

"I liked that dog."

"Did you . . . shoot him?"

"Right in the neck."

"He burned?"

"Only his arm hit the fire."

"But you let it burn?"

"He didn't feel it."

"Reeves, you're . . ."

Bass never found out what Webb was going to say. Webb closed his eyes and fell back.

He died just as the sun dropped below the edge of the horizon. Bass sat next to him for a while, wishing there was some wood to make a fire, wishing he was home, thinking of this, thinking of that, and then nothing.

Sighing, he stood and fetched Webb's horse and draped the body across the saddle, tying it in place, using a rein for a lead rope.

Then he mounted his gelding, turned around and started off. He'd have to walk Webb's horse until it could regain some strength. Twenty, twenty-five miles just to get back to where the run started. Then another hundred back to Fort Smith at a slow walk.

A long way home.

❧⊱✦⊰

Some arrests were very hard.

It took him ten days to get back to Fort Smith with Webb, and Bass needed to rest. He'd thought of it all the way back—just go sit at the ranch for a few days, maybe a week.

But when he entered Fort Smith, it did not seem the same place as when he had left. Men who would normally have stopped to pass the time moved across the street to get away from him.

Racial prejudice was always a problem for Bass, especially when he became the most successful deputy and was put in charge of white men who did not want to work under an African American. There had been a few incidents—minor problems, really—but his reputation was huge and so was he, six foot two when most men were five foot three or four.

128

He was aware of racial slurs. Today he thought that men were upset because he was the one who'd finally got Webb. But then he reconsidered—other deputies seemed to be afraid of him, for some reason. They would nod, give a tight little smile and move away quickly.

It made no sense. Most of them had always been sociable, and now there wasn't even the usual curiosity as to how he'd tracked and captured Webb.

At last he could stand it no more, and he cornered one of the senior deputies, a man named Leo Bennet. "What's wrong with everybody? They seem scared of me."

"They are," Bennet said, nodding. "I'm a little worried myself."

"What the hell are you talking about?"

"Let's walk a little," Bennet said. They were in front of the courthouse. "Away from other folks. I've got some bad news for you, Bass. Real bad. The worst there is."

They moved across the street to an empty spot. "What's happened is . . ." Bennet sighed. "I'd give almost anything not to have this conversation."

"What is it?"

"Your son Bennie. He murdered his wife and ran. He's out in the Territory, and Parker sent down a warrant on him. He had to. It's just sitting in there on the warrant bench. There wasn't a marshal or deputy here would touch it. They're all afraid of what you'd do to them if they had to . . . you know, shoot him."

Bass seemed to sag. "Bennie? My boy?"

After a moment, he took a breath, straightened. "It's certain he did it?"

Bennet hesitated, then nodded. "No doubt at all. He caught her with another man. After he did it, he yelled to witnesses that he had shot her for being unfaithful and that he would never come back alive."

"Damn fool kid . . ." Bass shook his head to clear it. He remembered his son as a small boy, smiling up at his father as they worked on the ranch side by side. That boy, now a cold-blooded killer. Bass felt the bile rise in his throat and sucked air through his teeth to fight the nausea.

"I'm sorry, Bass. Sorry as I can be. But we have to go after him. You know the rules."

Bass looked down the long street toward the gallows at the end. "I'll go get him."

Bennet shook his head. "God, Bass. You can't. What if he . . . what if it goes bad?"

"Then I'll do what has to be done. . . . I have to be the one who gets him. It's the only way he has a chance. With somebody else, he's sure to fight, and they will have to put him down. It has to be me. I can talk to him. I'll change horses and head out this afternoon. . . . Tell the other men even if they see him to not, you know . . ."

Bennet nodded. "Don't worry. They're too scared of you to come close to him."

"When did he . . . when did he leave?"

"Three days ago."

"Don't tell my wife. Leave that to me. When I get back, I'll . . ."

Bass walked away without finishing his sentence. He took two horses from his string at the livery barn, changed his saddle from the stallion—which, along with the geldings, needed at least a week of grain and good food to get weight back on—and after filling his canteen and stopping at the dry-goods store for coffee, bacon, cornmeal and jerky, he left Fort Smith. He hadn't been in town four hours. He had taken a big mare—a good distance horse and reliable when she wasn't in season—and he set out at a fast pace.

There was an urgency neither he nor Bennet had mentioned but that both men knew. Bennie was Bass Reeves's son. There were enough hard men in the Territory who hated Bass enough to take delight in killing his son, or capturing him for ransom.

Bass rode straight and hard all the rest of that day and through the night. As he rode, he steeled himself to put images of Bennie as a boy out of his mind. Bass had a sudden vivid mental image of Bennie when he was three years old. He was naked and standing in the yard holding on to the fur on the back of an old yard dog. Wherever the dog went, Bennie would run alongside, hanging on to the fur. It was just the cutest thing, Bass thought; Nellie would laugh and laugh, watching the little boy running in the dust naked, determined, his little hand gripping the fur as if he would never let go, never let go. . . .

God, he thought. Don't. Don't do this to me. Please. He tried not to picture his son at his wedding, his pretty dark-eyed bride, Tess. Bass allowed himself only once to wonder how his son, his boy, had wound up a killer. A killer . . . out here.

Bass turned his attention to the job that lay ahead and told himself that he was going after a criminal just like any other. Nothing more. It was his son, but it was still a chase, and he was still Bass Reeves. He rode, dry-eyed, the rest of the night.

He got to the store at Miller's Crossing. Fat old Ben

Grist owned the store—if a shack that sold hardly anything but whiskey could be called a store—and he was usually drunk enough to be talkative. If not, he could be urged to talk. And Bass was in a mood where urging wouldn't be a problem for him.

Grist was ready. "The kid come through here two, no, three days ago," he said through a beard fouled with food and whiskey and tobacco spit. "On a sorrel gelding, had run him until he looked like he was covered in lye soap. Never saw a horse so lathered up."

"Which way did he go?"

"Started west, but I come out and watched, and as soon as he was down the trail a mite, he turned and moved north. Up into that break country. You'll never find him up there. No, sir, you won't get that one. He got clean away."

Bass ignored him, moved outside and remounted and headed north. It was rough country up north but old man Grist had been wrong. The break country was all bad gullies and sharp little rocky canyons—so rough it left only a limited number of places you could take a horse. If Bennie had gone in there, Bass would find him. Bass had lived in the breaks for months when he was a fugitive and knew every nook and cranny.

It was just a matter of time now, time and patience. He worked up into the breaks with care, saving his horse.

As he rode, he thought back to the witch dog long ago. "Things will change." Of course, Bass's whole life had been full of change. But this mission . . . yes, things had changed in the most terrible way.

On the fourth day, he found him.

He found the tracks of a single horse just after daybreak. Once the mare saw they were following the tracks,

132

he let her have her way and scanned ahead. They were in an area of small, sharp-walled rocky canyons where the experienced criminals never hid because they knew it was a trap; the only way out was the way they'd come in.

But Bennie had never been an outlaw and didn't think that way. In one of the small canyons Bass came around a bend and saw a rock-walled shack that had been abandoned by homesteaders long ago. Bennie's horse was hobbled out in some grass to the right.

He rode straight in, stopped in front of the shack, dismounted and called, "You got coffee on?"

He heard footsteps scrambling, and then the old door opened. Bennie was holding a gun, but when he saw Bass, he put it down against the inside wall. "I knew you'd be the one to come."

"It had to be me. It was the only way."

"I don't have any coffee."

"I've got some." Bass took the coffee and a pot out of his saddlebag and handed them to Bennie. "Put some on while I hobble my mare."

Bass heard Bennie rattling a stove lid and then a fire starting. He dealt with the mare and then sat down next to the shack on a big rock in the sun. He had never smoked and now he wished he had started, just to have something to do with his hands.

"What am I going to do, Pa?" Bennie had come back out. "What's going to happen?"

"You have to go back and stand for it."

"But I caught her. She was right there and—"

"It don't matter. You've got to stand for it."

"But why?"

"Because," Bass said, sighing, looking out across the

grass, looking at everything, looking at nothing, past the edge of the world. "Because it's the law."

He paused and looked up to study his son. "The law. It's not just the white man's rules anymore, son, and free men live by the law."

Epilogue

Bass brought his son Bennie back to stand trial and stood by him through it all, stood by him when he was found guilty and when he was sentenced to life in prison. (After serving an unspecified time as a model prisoner, Bennie was pardoned and released. He lived a straightforward and successful life for his remaining years.)

Bringing his son in did not break Bass. It is hard to believe that anything could break him—but he later said it was the hardest thing he had ever done.

In 1907, law enforcement in the Territory was taken away from the federal marshals and turned over to the individual communities. Muskogee, Oklahoma, still very much a wild and woolly Western town, approached Bass and asked him to be the town constable.

At age eighty-one, he accepted the job. Such was his

reputation and hard work that from 1907 to 1909 not a single crime was committed on his beat.

In late 1909 his health began to fail, and he died on January 12, 1910, of Bright's disease.

The *Muskogee Phoenix* wrote:

"Bass Reeves is dead. He passed away yesterday afternoon . . . and in a short time news of his death had reached the federal courthouse where it recalled to the officers and clerks many incidents in the early days of the United States in which the old . . . deputy figured heroically.

"Everybody who came in contact with the . . . deputy in an official capacity had a great deal of respect for him, and at the court house in Muskogee one can hear stories of his devotion to duty, his unflinching courage and his many thrilling experiences. . . . At different times his belt was shot in two, a button shot off his coat, his hat brim shot off and the bridle rein in his hand cut by a bullet. However, in spite of all these narrow escapes and the many conflicts in which he was engaged . . . he killed fourteen men . . . Reeves was never wounded. And this, notwithstanding the fact that he never fired a shot until the desperado he was trying to arrest had started the shooting."

❖

Each year thousands of tourists and curiosity seekers go to the grave of Billy the Kid in Fort Sumter, New Mexico. Many pray and weep and some even worship at the grave, thinking Billy was an innocent youth.

The same thing happens in Deadwood, South Dakota, where Wild Bill Hickok is buried. People weep at what they think is the tragic loss of an American hero.

Mourners and tourists flock to Lookout Mountain above

Golden, Colorado, to the grave of William F. Cody, and thousands visit the grave of Kit Carson, in Taos, New Mexico. Mobs stop in Tombstone, Arizona, every year just to see the place of the gunfight at the OK Corral. And there's a cult of people who want to know what "really" happened to Butch Cassidy and the Sundance Kid.

There is nothing for Bass Reeves. He lies in an unknown place in an unmarked grave, ignored by dime novelists in his lifetime and by Hollywood after his death. There are no monuments to him, no flocks of weeping tourists, no epic films or drums or music, no last words or sweeping eternal thoughts.

He was there.

And then he was gone.

But perhaps there is a suitable epitaph for him, spoken by a man who worked with him and knew his character. When some doubter asked Chief Marshal Leo Bennet about Bass, and what qualities he had that made him worth keeping as a deputy, Bennet looked at the man and said:

"He never shirked his duty."

ABOUT THE AUTHOR

Gary Paulsen is the distinguished author of many critically acclaimed books for young people, including three Newbery Honor books: *The Winter Room, Hatchet,* and *Dogsong.* His novel *The Haymeadow* received the Western Writers of America Golden Spur Award. Among his Random House books are *The Time Hackers; Molly McGinty Has a Really Good Day; The Quilt* (a companion to *Alida's Song* and *The Cookcamp); The Glass Café; How Angel Peterson Got His Name; Caught by the Sea: My Life on Boats; Guts: The True Stories Behind* Hatchet *and the Brian Books; The Beet Fields; Soldier's Heart; Brian's Return, Brian's Winter,* and *Brian's Hunt* (companions to *Hatchet); Father Water, Mother Woods;* and five books about Francis Tucket's adventures in the Old West. Gary Paulsen has also published fiction and nonfiction for adults, as well as picture books illustrated by his wife, the painter Ruth Wright Paulsen. Their most recent book is *Canoe Days.* The Paulsens live in New Mexico, in Alaska, and on the Pacific Ocean.